DEATH WISH

AN AL PENNYBACK
MYSTERY

CHARLES RAY

North Potomac, MD

Death Wish

DEDICATION

To the victims of the September 11, 2001 attacks, and the valiant first responders who risked – and in many cases gave – their lives to try to save others. And, a special note of gratitude to the men and women of the armed forces and our civilian agencies who have sacrificed so much in the wars in Afghanistan and Iraq, and who continue to stand guard over the freedoms that the rest of us often take for granted. Their sacrifices prove beyond a shadow of a doubt that 'Freedom is not Free,' it's paid for by the blood of patriots.

1.

Ten days after it happened, the city – the country – was still in a state of shock.

Who would have thought it possible that anyone would hijack civilian airliners filled with passengers and fly them into occupied buildings?

But, it had happened, and the reaction was, first disbelief, then shock, then anger. Politicians made speeches, some called for war, and I noticed that the loudest voices calling for an armed response, an attack on someone in retaliation for this heinous act, came from those politicians who had never worn a uniform or had a shot fired at them in anger.

Armed guards in combat gear were now around every government building in the DC area, and getting into buildings, even those with no real secrets to protect, was time-consuming and hardly worth the effort. I didn't fly, but Quincy Chang, my friend and a senior partner in the law firm that had me on retainer, had to fly a lot in his work, and he'd told me that when airlines were permitted to fly again after September 11, the security checks were extensive, exhaustive, and embarrassing – but, in his view, not all that effective, designed more to reassure the flying public that the government was taking decisive action than to actually deter a determined hijacker.

I was as shocked at what had happened as anyone, but I had to make a living, so I tried to put the events behind me and get on with my life. It wasn't easy. I'd known some of the 125 people who'd died in the Pentagon when American Airlines flight 77, bound to Los Angeles from Dulles International Airport, had been turned around and crashed into the building at 9:37 that morning.

Increased security checks at all of the military installations in the DC area had impacted me a little. I mean, I understood their concern, and I have no objection to measures to keep people on an installation or in a building safe, but having to raise my hood and trunk every time I entered Fort McNair to go to the Officer's Club for lunch was a huge pain in the ass. Especially, since I had my military retiree ID card, and had been visiting the base for more than ten years. I decided that until things calmed down and people came to their senses, I'd just eat at the nearest Burger King.

Military personnel were on full alert, pulling long hours and being mostly confined to their places of duty. So, it came as a surprise when

Colonel William Raymond called my office and asked to meet me at Adugna, an Ethiopian restaurant on Arlington Pike southwest of the Pentagon. He was quiet and rushed on the phone, as if someone might be listening in and he didn't want them to hear. I wasn't surprised that he hadn't invited me to meet him at the Pentagon cafeteria in the basement. The place would probably still be blocked off for repairs caused by the plane, which had penetrated the ground floor of the building on the west side from the outer E Ring all the way in to the C Ring. I still knew a lot of people working in the building, and occasionally met them for lunch – at the Pentagon, or at one of the nearby bases, like Ft. Myer in Arlington or Ft. McNair in the District, so it was unusual that Raymond wouldn't chose one of them.

I decided not to press the issue, though. He sounded really worried, worried enough to pique my curiosity.

William Raymond had been a second lieutenant when I first met him. An infantry officer, he'd been a platoon leader in the First Infantry Division in Korea assigned to be aggressor against my Special Forces team during a special exercise. We'd whipped their asses soundly, and the young commander, rather than being pissed at us as many regular guys were when we aced them in exercises, had invited my team and me to the Division officer club for drinks. I'd run into him later at Ft. Bragg after he was promoted to captain and accepted into Special Forces training. We ran into each other from time to time after he graduated and was assigned to one of the A teams at Bragg, but because I was on special assignment to do highly sensitive missions, our contacts were infrequent.

We hadn't seen much of each other since Raymond was assigned to the Pentagon; I wasn't even sure what his job was there. I didn't think, however, that he just wanted to talk about old times.

The call had come in to my office at 10:30, and he'd asked to meet at noon. Figuring a thirty minute drive in traffic from my office on Fourth Street in Southwest DC, I got in my green Volkswagen bug at 11:15 and headed up Fourth to Maine Avenue and then across the Potomac River on the Fourteenth Street Bridge. Traffic on the way out of the city was light, so I made good time to the Washington Boulevard exit and then west on Columbia Pike.

Despite knowing what had happened to the Pentagon, I was unprepared for the large canvas screen they'd erected on the south face, covering the gaping maw where the Boeing 757 had bounced off the parking lot and smashed into it, burrowing over 300 feet into the building's interior. I'd seen bomb damage before, but there was something about this that hit me in the gut like a mule kick.

I felt better when the road dipped as I approached Columbia Pike, and I could no longer see the Pentagon. Once on Columbia

Pike and heading generally southwest, things looked normal.

The parking lot at Adugna was only sparsely populated with cars, which didn't surprise me, as most of the people who ate at the ethnic restaurants along Columbia Pike walked from nearby apartments, or worked in one of the strip malls that dotted the pike all the way to Annandale. I parked near the building and went in.

Unlike the parking lot, the inside of Adugna was crowded. The lunch crowd was out in full force. The odor of ginger, pepper, lamb cooking, and human sweat slammed into my face as I entered the large dimly lit dining room. I felt a slight wooziness. I wasn't sure which smell was doing it, either, the lamb or the sweaty bodies – both were pungent and off-putting.

Most of the patrons looked to be Ethiopian, with a scattering of swarthy Hispanic faces in the crowd. Raymond, even though he wore casual civilian clothes, stood out like a candle in a dark room. I spotted his fair skin and ash blond buzz cut hair from across the room.

He sat at a table in the back in a corner. There were only two chairs, both backed on the walls. He sat in the one on the right, scanning the room slowly. He caught sight of me as soon as I walked through the door, but made no move to indicate it other than a slight lift of his eyebrows and a brief pause in his scanning as our gazes locked. As I neared, he stopped scanning the room and looked up at me, a slight smile on his face. He inclined his head to indicate that I should take the empty chair.

After I sat down, he extended his hand. We shook briefly.

"Thanks for coming, Colonel," he said.

"It's just Al, these days," I said. "You're the colonel."

His smile broadened. "Old habits die hard. I remember you as one tough-as-nails Special Forces light colonel who I'd never dare address by his first name."

"Those days are far behind me," I said. "I'm just a lowly PI now, so, call me Al."

"Okay, Al," he said. "My friends call me Bill. I hope you don't mind Ethiopian food. I kind of developed a taste for it when I did a training mission with the Ethiopians in Addis a few years ago." He fiddled with the acetate-covered menu as his head resumed its side to side swivel. He was keeping a close eye on everyone in the place, and he seemed nervous. "I think you'll like it, although the *injera*, that's a kind of fermented flat bread, is an acquired taste. They have a pretty wide variety of dishes . . . lamb, or beef if you prefer. I seem to remember from Bragg, that you're not fond of lamb. Lots of vegetables and noodles, and everything is spiced with *berbere,* a mixture of ground chili pepper, ginger, garlic, coriander, and about eighteen or so other spices."

He *was* nervous. We hadn't exactly been running buddies, but he knew that anyone who'd been in Special Forces didn't need a lecture on local cuisine. We'd been trained to eat whatever was put in front of us, and never inquire about the contents.

"You're right about the lamb," I said. "Never developed a taste for it, but I'm okay with everything else." I picked up the second menu and opened it. "I'm curious, though, why'd you want to see me? I figured you guys in the Pentagon would be pretty bush with the aftermath of the attacks right now."

The military response, in addition to heightened security at installations, had been robust. Fighter jets crisscrossed the sky over DC at all hours. Most of the area's residents probably didn't notice, because they flew pretty high, but there was no mistaking the whine of high performance engines or the tic-tac-toe pattern of contrails in the sky.

He stopped fiddling with the menu and looked intently across the table at me. Something was on his mind, that much was plain to see, but I hadn't a clue what it could be. Finally, he sighed and cupped his hands together, resting them on the menu.

"Al, I have a problem . . . a doozy of a problem, and I think you're the only person I to help me with it."

"What kind of problem could an army colonel have that only I could help with? I'm a private investigator," I said. "I don't do divorce cases."

He laughed. "Damn, I wish is was that simple. It's not that kind of case. It involves my work at the Pentagon."

Warning bells started clanging in my head. I usually try to avoid getting tangled up with the government. The last few times I got involved with federal matters, things didn't end well.

"I think you're knocking on the wrong door, Bill," I said. "I do skip chase work for a law firm, and take the occasional case that the cops can't or won't deal with. You got the Defense Investigative Service and the Army's Criminal Investigation Division to tap. If it's job related, why don't you take it to one of them?"

"I wish I could," he said. "But, since 9-11, everyone in uniform's been focused solely on fighting terrorists. I can't get any of the brass to take this particular problem seriously."

"Does this particular problem involve illegal activity?"

"That's part of the problem." He rubbed at his jaw. "I'm not sure. I think it might . . . the person who brought it to my attention thinks so, and I trust him. But, I don't have any hard evidence, so when I took it to my boss, he told me to drop it."

Dammit, I thought. I have no business sticking my nose in government business. But, Raymond was a straight shooter in my book, and if he felt something bad was going down, my gut told me to believe him. He was presenting me with a puzzle, and I'm a sucker for a puzzle. He'd also informed me that the high muck-a-mucks were looking down their noses at it, and I'd never been a great fan of the big brass. I could hear the sucking sounds of myself being pulled into his mess.

"Okay, why don't you tell me the nature of this illegal activity," I said.

2.

He leaned forward, his elbows on the table. "I work in the Joint Staff Office of Project Development," he said. "We're responsible for overseeing new weapons platforms. One of the contractors we're working with, Armcor, is supposed to be developing an unmanned armed aerial reconnaissance vehicle. The on-site project manager is a sharp young noncom, Staff Sergeant Rory Lake. He came to me a week ago to report his suspicions that Armcor's executives are fudging the figures on the performance of their prototype."

"Whoa, back up," I said. "That's a lot of description in one sentence. What the hell is an unmanned . . .?"

"It's basically an unmanned aerial vehicle or UAV . . . some people call them drones . . . used primarily for reconnaissance over hostile territory. This one, though, will be armed and capable of missile strikes on selected targets."

"Sort of like the drones we used in

Vietnam?" I remembered the lumbering devices that had been designed to hit the North Vietnamese infiltrating along the Ho Chi Minh Trail. They'd loiter around an area, but often, by the time the authorization for a strike came down the chain of command, the target would be long gone.

Raymond chuckled. "The new generation of . . . drones is to the ones you remember from Vietnam what an ICBM is to a slingshot," he said. "We've built on what the Israelis have done with their UAV program, and with some of the new technology, these things are like unmanned airplanes." He looked around, and lowered his voice. "They can be flown over targets in places like the Middle East by a pilot sitting in an air conditioned control room here in the United States."

"Holy shit," I said. "That'll change the hell out of the way we fight wars."

He opened his mouth to speak, but snapped it shut when the waitress, a cute young Ethiopian girl whose breasts and hips looked like they would burst through the tight dress she wore at her next step, approached our table.

I let him order for the both of us, after pointing out that I don't eat sheep – mutton, lamb chops, whatever, I just can't quite deal with the greasiness. He ordered *Maheberawi*, a mixed meat plate containing beef stew, goat cubes, and raw ground beef. He assured me that this would be more than enough for the two of us, as it would contain several *injera,* or flatbread pancakes which we would use instead of utensils to eat the rest. He then ordered Italian espresso coffee.

"I would order traditional Ethiopian coffee," he said. "But, that would mean the waitress would be at the table for twenty minutes or more, preparing the beans and brewing it, and I'd like a little privacy. The espresso's pretty good, though. Probably the only decent thing the Italians left during their brief attempt at colonizing Ethiopia."

The girl bowed and smiled, and withdrew to get out food. "Now, you were saying these new drones will change the way we fight," he said. "You're partially right. There are a few people in the Pentagon who fear it will make it too easy for us to get involved in conflicts, and being able to strike targets remotely might erode our commitment to the rules of war. But, at the end of the day, it'll still take boots on the ground to defeat the enemy."

"Are you one of those people?"

He looked at me for a long time before he spoke. "I'm not sure sometimes, Al. War is serious business. If we turn it into a video game, I guess I worry we'll raise a generation of youngsters who don't realize just how bloody it really is."

"Okay, I just had to ask," I said. "But, what does that have to do with me? Or, put another way, how in hell is a private detective related to drone warfare?"

"You're not, at least not directly." He paused again as the waitress brought our coffee, and then a few minutes later brought a large plate upon which was enough food to feed four people. He waited until she was back across the room to continue. "It's Armcor that I need your help on. Sergeant Lake told me he thinks they're fudging their numbers and claiming capabilities for their prototype that it doesn't possess. But, I can't get the brass to take it seriously enough to officially look into it."

"So, you want me to investigate a major defense contractor?"

He picked up one of the circles of flat bread and broke off a piece the size of a playing card. He then used it to scoop up some brown meat cubes that he said were goat meat. I copied him. It was spicy, with a hint of ginger, and quite good. We washed the first bites down with espresso. When I sighed in satisfaction at the taste, he continued talking.

"Armcor is not really what you'd call a major contractor," he said. "In fact, until they got this contract, the company was barely getting by. I'm not even sure how they got the damn contract in the first place. They have no experience building aerial vehicles."

"Sounds like they have some pretty powerful juice with someone in DOD," I said.

"Yeah, but I can't figure out who. Anyway, when Lake came to me, I took it to General Bennington, that's Brigadier General Frank Bennington, the head of my division. He said he'd look into it, but then the damn jihadis flew those planes into the Trade Center buildings and the Pentagon, and his attention was diverted."

"I can see that," I said. "At least for the first few days, but his job's to oversee contracts, not fight terrorists. Shouldn't he have paid attention after a while?"

He stopped chewing, and spoke around a mouth half full of food. "That's what I thought." He swallowed. "I spent the whole weekend and the first few days of the week thinking about it, and when I went in to see him yesterday, he told me to drop it, to forget about the whole matter."

"Did he give you a reason for dropping it?"

"No, that's the problem." He shook his head. "Well, that's part of the problem. He didn't even want to discuss it, and that's not like him."

I didn't want to argue with him, but my experience with senior people, in or out of uniform, was that often their positions went to their heads, replacing whatever common sense they might have had.

"Why didn't you take this . . . Sergeant Lake in? Let him tell his story. Maybe that would have changed the general's mind."

"I thought about that," he said. "But, that's my other problem. Sergeant Lake seems to have disappeared."

"Disappeared? How can that be? Doesn't he have to report in to his unit from time to time?"

"Sure, he's supposed to check in every three

days, but I haven't heard from him since last Friday. He didn't check in Wednesday like he was supposed to, and he's not answering his phone. I went by his house last night. His car was in the driveway, but there were no lights on in the house, and no one answered the bell."

That didn't sound good, not good at all.

"Does he have any relatives or friends he might be staying with? Is it possible he's gone AWOL?"

"No to both," he said. "He was an only child, and both of his parents died when he was seventeen, that's when he joined the army. As for going AWOL, that makes no sense. Lake was on the fast track for promotion; he doesn't drink, and has no reason to do something that stupid. No, I think something's happened to him."

"And, you think it's connected to Armcor?"

"Al, I don't know what to think. I know I've been told to stay away from Armcor. Look, I can pay you for your time. I really need your help on this."

"Have you reported Lake missing . . . to the military, or to the local cops?"

He shook his head. "No, until I know what's going on, I didn't want to make a big deal of it. If I report him missing, Bennington's likely to list him as AWOL, and that could screw his career. Since Lake reports to me, no one else knows about this – except, now you. I need you to find him, and see if you can find out what Armcor's up to while you're at it."

Things had been slow around the office. Quincy's law firm hadn't had too many cases for me to work, and nothing had come over the transom, so I had the time to work his case. Besides, it was beginning to interest me.

"Okay, I'll take it on. I'll have my assistant do up a contract and she'll handle any funds transfers. I assume you don't want us calling you at your office?"

"That's for sure." He took a pad from his shirt and wrote a number on it. "This is my cell number, but only call me on it after seven in the evening. If you or your assistant have to meet me in person, call the day before, and I'll arrange a rendezvous."

This was beginning to sound like some kind of undercover intelligence operation, but I imagine he worried about the damage to his career if his boss found out he was disobeying orders.

"Okay," I said. "I need Lake's address, and anything you can give me on Armcor. I'll get started right away."

He wrote down an address in Alexandria, near Huntington Metro station a working class neighborhood where the sergeant rented a house. Armcor's offices were in a high rise on Twenty-Third Street in Crystal City, not far from the Metro Towers. I took the paper, folded it, and put it in my shirt pocket.

I decided to start by trying to track the sergeant down. It was already after 1:30, and that late on Friday, I wasn't likely to get much from Armcor.

We finished our meal in silence, and he stayed behind to let me leave first so no one outside the place would see us together.

3.

I was back in my office by 3:00. Heather was at her computer, which is where she usually is. She was busy pecking away at the keyboard when I walked in.

"Banker's hours again," she said. "You said you were meeting some guy from the Pentagon. I didn't know the buttoned down military types went in for late lunches."

There was a bit of teasing in her voice. She loves busting my chops. Now that we were full partners, she did it even more than she did when she was just my lowly paid assistant. Of course, I got my own licks in from time to time. For instance, I occasionally called her Honeybunch, which was a play on her name, Heather Bunche, and the fact that with her close-cropped blonde hair and diminutive size, she looked like a little pixie. It was all in fun, though. We'd been doing it for more than ten years, from the beginning, after I'd let Quincy Chang talk me into getting my PI license and opening up shop. I'm lousy at paperwork, and she'd just graduated from secretarial school and needed a job. She was a whiz at paperwork, and it turned out something of a computer expert as well, so it had worked perfectly for the both of us.

"We have a new client," I said. I gave her the details for a contract, and the contact number.

"That's a new one. With all the resources of the Defense Department, this guy needs us?"

I explained his fears and pointed out that the military types were currently more concerned with hunting down terrorists than nabbing crooked contractors. "You have to remember, Honeybunch," I said. "You're dealing with pretty straight forward, one dimensional minds here. These guys can only deal with one problem at a time. There's also the problem of Sergeant Lake. The first thing they're likely to do in his case is declare him AWOL. If he is in trouble, that won't help."

Her beautiful face scrunched up in a concerned look. "I see. Okay, what do you want me to do?"

"I want you to do what you do best," I said. "I'd like you to find out everything there is to know about Armcor; what they do, where they do it, who owns the place; but, most importantly, I want to know if they have any skeletons in their closets."

She pulled a pad from her desk and began making notes in her precise handwriting. "You think they're up to no good?"

"Bill Raymond said the missing sergeant thought they were up to something. I don't know the sergeant, but I do know Raymond, and he trusted the sergeant, so for now, that's good enough for me."

She stopped writing and looked at me over the top of the pad, which blocked the view of the lower half of her face. "You know, of course," she said. "These guys will have more firewalls around their data than even the government, because they protect it against competitors. And, if they're involved in anything shady, there's likely to be even more security."

"I trust you to find a way past their walls," I said. I chuckled. "You always seem to be able to do that."

"And, if I can't?"

She made a good point. If she couldn't get to them through their computers, that might present a problem.

"We'll breech that firewall when we come to it," I said.

Her face took on a pained expression at my lame attempt at a pun. Hey, I'm a PI, not a comedian.

I decided to use the rest of the day to see what I could find out about Rory Lake, so I left her pecking away at her keyboard again, and went back to the Bug for a little ground reconnaissance.

I took the U.S. Highway 1 south off ramp from the Fourteenth Street Bridge, and drove through Crystal City and Old Town Alexandria, one a stretch of expensive hotels, glitzy department stores, trendy condos, and office towers, the second mostly brownstone office buildings and stores, with a sprinkling of townhouses. When the highway goes under I-495, the surroundings change. On the left, between the highway and the Potomac River is an area of old money. Large mansions set back from the road and surrounded by towering oaks. On the right are derelict warehouses and abandoned factories. This lasts for about three quarters of a mile, and then you hit what I call suburban Virginia strip mall country.

This is area that's not quite rural, but not totally suburban either, and with no apparent zoning restrictions. One area will contain a nice looking motel with landscaped grounds across the street from a steel frame building that rebuilds diesel engines. The farther you get away from Alexandria, heading in the direction of Fort Belvoir, home to the U.S. Army's engineer school for a long time, the more you see liquor stores, pawn shops, malls – large and small - and road side bars. Stuck among all this commercial activity, seemingly at random, are housing areas, ranging from fairly new brick or concrete apartments to old wood frame houses.

Rory Lake rented a small house in one of the wood frame neighborhoods. Located on Madison Street, a small, two-lane blacktop street east off Highway 1, it was a community that had been built before homeowners associations began to proliferate in the Washington area. Every house was different from its neighbors, and reflected its owner or occupant's pride or lack thereof. There were a few large dwellings, but most were about the size of a two-car garage, or in some cases, two two-car garages, one atop the other. Dark squares on many of the roofs showed where shingles had been blown off and not replaced. A tiny percentage of the houses were constructed of mildew-covered red brick, but most were wood frame with scaly areas where the paint had begun peeling off.

Lake lived in a one-story dirty gray house with a dusty looking green shingle roof that set back a bit farther from the street than any of its neighbors. The drive way was basically two tire tracks cut into an unkempt lawn and ending at a rusty gate that hung askew in a rustier chain link fence that enclosed the side and back yards. A silver Dodge Ram pickup sat with its front bumper against the gate. I pulled in behind the pickup and killed the engine.

As I got out of the car, a tiny woman wearing an ankle length skirt with an oversized blouse untucked came out of the back door of the two story house next door. She stopped on the steps and stared at me for a few minutes, and then she stepped to the ground and started in my direction with a determined look on her face. Curious, I stopped and waited for her.

"Hi," she said, as she neared me. "You looking for Mr. Lake?" She looked me up and down suspiciously.

"Yes, I am," I said. I started for the front door.

She followed me. "I don't think he's home."

I stopped and turned to face her.

"His truck's parked here," I said.

She gave me a peevish look. "I can see that, but *he's* not here."

I decided to play along with her. Maybe she'd go away and I could get on with my investigation.

"How do you know he's not here?"

"Because I saw him leave with his friend, and he hasn't come back."

There was a note of triumph in her voice, and she had an 'I told you so' look on her thin face. I felt like I had egg on mine.

"When did you see him leave?" When you've been embarrassed, the best thing to do is take the offensive.

"Last Friday night . . . no, Saturday morning," she said.

"Which was it, Friday night or Saturday morning?" I gave her my best patronizing smile.

"It was just after midnight Friday, so that made it Saturday," she said, ignoring my attempt to put her down. "Why are you looking for him? You some kind of creditor or something?"

She was now looking at me as if she was just about to turn around, run back into her house, and call 911. The last thing I wanted at this point in the investigation was to have to deal with nosy local cops.

"I'm a private investigator," I said. I took my ID out and showed it to her. "Sergeant Lake is being considered for a very important job, and I've been hired to do a background check on him."

I banked on her not knowing that the military did its own background investigations. The way her eyebrows went up, I thought she was close to buying my story.

"Shouldn't you be talking to other people before you talk to him?"

She was no dummy. I'd have to tread carefully with her. "Ordinarily we do," I said. "But, I wanted to get a look at his living situation. Now that I have you here, though, would you mind talking to me about him?"

The eyebrows went down to their normal position, and the ends of her mouth turned up in a smile. Of course, she'd be willing to talk to me.

"What do you want to know?" she asked.

Now, we were getting somewhere – maybe. I took my note pad and pen from my pocket.

"Let's start with your name and how long you've known Sergeant Lake," I said.

"Wouldn't it be better to do this inside?" She frowned at me. "I just made a pot of tea. Would you like a cup?"

Without waiting for me to agree, she turned and walked back to her house. After mounting the steps to the back door, she turned and looked at me impatiently. I shrugged and followed.

She led me into a small kitchen that had a small wooden table with two chairs in the corner near the window. A ceramic tea pot sat in the center of the table. Next to it was a fancy looking china cup and saucer. She motioned me to the chair nearest the window, and went to the cabinet over the sink and got another cup and saucer. She came back to the table and sat in the chair facing the window and poured tea into the cup, and then slid it across the table to me.

"Would you like cream and sugar with that?" she asked. I shook my head. She smiled. "Good, that's the way tea should be drunk. Never understood why people would want to ruin the taste with milk and sugar anyway." She took a sip of hers, smacked her lips and put the cup down. "Now, you asked my name . . . it's Lorraine Zeller, and I've known Mr., uh, Sergeant Lake . . . let's see, he moved in about eighteen months ago. Came over the first day and introduced himself. A real polite young man, he is. Not many of his generation are polite like that."

As she talked I noticed something that had escaped my attention outside. She had a network of fine lines at the corner of her eyes, the beginning of a wattle under her chin, and a sprinkling of liver spots on the backs of her hands. She was older than I would have first guessed. From the way she looked over my shoulder through the window behind me, it was also clear that she had little to occupy her time besides keeping track of what went on in the neighborhood. That made her a good, if not necessarily reliable, source of information.

"In the time you've known him, have you ever seen Sergeant Lake do anything strange?"

"What do you mean by strange?"

"Oh, drinking to excess, doing drugs, things like that."

Her frown deepened. "No, I've never seen him do anything like that," she said. "Like I told you, he's a very polite young man, no late night parties or noise, no empty beer cans or liquor bottles in his trash. He kept pretty much to himself . . . until the last month."

I stopped pretending to write. "What changed in the past month?"

"Well, that friend of his started coming around every few days," she said. Her brow wrinkled, and she frowned. "I don't like to judge people, and he never did anything bad that I saw, but he just made me nervous."

I leaned forward. "What was it about him made you nervous?"

She shook her head, and put a hand to her brow. "I-I can't really say," she said. "There was just something menacing about him. I never could see why Rory, uh, Sergeant Lake, let him hang around."

"What was this friend's name?"

She looked puzzled. "Uh, that's strange. I never thought about it before, but he never introduced himself, and Rory never talked about him."

That was strange. Lorraine Zeller struck me as the type who dug information out of people just to pass the time. That Lake hadn't shared information about him with her seemed to me to be a deliberate oversight. The question was, why?

"What can you tell me about Friday night?"

"Not much," she said. "Rory came home around six in the evening. I was just picking some peppers off my plants out back, and he said hello. He went inside like he usually does." She took a sip of tea. "That man . . . came around eleven. I couldn't sleep, you see, so I was sitting here drinking tea. Rory let him in, and then around midnight, they left together."

"I take it they left in the man's car," I said. "Do you remember what kind of car it was?"

"I don't know anything about cars. It's a big, black SUV is all I know."

"And, Sergeant Lake . . . Rory, hasn't been back home since Friday?"

"No," she said. "I'd know if he came back."

That didn't leave me anything else to ask her really. It did, however, present me with a deepening puzzle. "Okay, Ms. Zeller," I said. "Thank you very much for your cooperation." I gave her one of my name cards. "If you think of anything else, or you hear from Rory, would you please call me?"

She put the card to one side. "I sure will. Are you going to talk to anyone else in the neighborhood?"

"No, I think as his next door neighbor, you're probably the best source of information here." That brought a bright smile. I was serious, though. "Thanks for your time."

I finished my tea and left. On the way to my car, I circled Lake's house, peering into the windows. The place looked as deserted as Zeller had claimed. I saw an unwashed plate and glass on the kitchen sink, but couldn't get a clear look at it. As I got in my car I saw Lorraine Zeller watching me from her kitchen window.

Charles Ray

4.

On my way home, I called Heather. I had to stop her from giving me a data dump over the phone. I told her she could hold it until Monday.

It was nearly six when I arrived at the farm house I own off River Road west of Potomac Village in Montgomery County, Maryland. I'd lived alone for the first few years after I bought the place at an estate sale, but for the past four years Sandra Winter, a teacher at Carter High School in the District who I'd met when I was investigating the murder of one of her students had been living with me. She had a house in the District, in Takoma Park, which she'd finally moved her stuff out of and rented out.

Ours was a mutually convenient relationship. We were fond of each other – one could go so far as to say that we loved each other – but, we were content to let the relationship develop at its own pace.

Sandra had beaten me home by several

hours. We'd agreed that morning to make an evening of it, so when I walked in, she was sitting on the sofa already dressed and ready to roll.

"Sorry I'm late, babe," I said. "Give me a few minutes to wash the sweat off and change."

She stood up, leaned forward, and gave me a peck on the cheek. "You get a proper kiss when you've cleaned up," she said.

I didn't argue. Sandra is a couple inches shorter than my six-one, as athletic as hell, and I've been teaching her taekwondo for a couple of years, and she's about ready to take me down. Besides, the weather had been warm for September, and I sweat a lot, so if I'd been in her place I would have treated me the same way.

It took me about thirty minutes to shower, run a razor over my five o'clock shadow, and pull on a pair of blue dress pants, a blue cotton dress shirt, and a dark blue dress jacket over that. I buffed my best black dress shoes with an old rag I keep in the back of the closet, spritzed myself with a mist of Aqua Velva, and went back to the living room.

"Do I pass inspection?" I asked, doing a little pirouette in front of the sofa.

She cupped my face in her hands and kissed me full on the lips, pressing her body against mine. I slipped my arms around her waist, pulling her in even closer. After what felt like it was far too short a time, she pulled back. "We'd better stop this, or we'll never get dinner."

I made a growling sound deep in my throat. "Okay," I said. "But, you owe me."

We took my car, leaving her little Honda parked in the front yard. As we drove away, I made a mental note to cut the grass which was getting a bit shaggy. I drove down River Road and took a right onto Seven Locks Road near the Beltway. Seven Locks ends at MacArthur Boulevard, and we went left on MacArthur into the District, turned onto Reservoir Road and drove down past the Georgetown University campus to M Street. Just past the old locomotive garage that now serves as ROTC headquarters at Georgetown I crossed Key Bridge into Rosslyn on Fort Myer Boulevard. In the heart of Rosslyn, we turned right onto Wilson Boulevard and drove about three miles southwest to a small shopping mall on the right that contained a pawn shop, a video rental shop, and three restaurants – Vietnamese, Cambodian, and Thai. We decided to try *Loy Krathong*, the Thai restaurant.

The place was small and dimly lit. Most of the patrons were Asian, with a few white couples scattered about. A diminutive Thai waitress greeted us at the door and led us to a table for two in the back near the bar. We ordered two *Singha* beers, and she left the menus for us to peruse while she went to get out drinks.

"What are you in the mood for?" I asked Sandra. "Spicy or mild?"

"Not too spicy," she said. "I like that green

salad dish we had the last time we ate Thai."

She was referring to the green papaya salad, *som tam*, which was also one of my favorites.

"Yeah, I like *som tam* too. And, I think some spicy chicken soup and red curry with rice will go well with it," I said.

"Sounds good. Here comes the waitress," she said.

The waitress put our beers on the table and took out her pad to take our food order. My Thai is really rusty, but she smiled and didn't make fun of me as I ordered *som tam, tom yam gai,* and *gaeng curry* with rice.

The nice thing about Thai food is it doesn't take long from pot to plate, so we didn't have time for much conversation before the waitress was setting bowls and plates in the center of the table. She put an empty plate in front of each of us along with a fork and spoon. We would be eating in traditional Thai style, serving ourselves from the communal containers in the center of the table and using a fork and spoon rather than the chopsticks common to many other Asian cuisines.

When we'd gotten a goodly amount of rice and other ingredients on our plates, I took a sip of beer and then put a spoonful of rice and curry in my mouth. The curry was spicy, not too spicy, just a little bite. Sandra was more tentative, but as the sweet, sour and spicy taste of the curry hit her taste buds, she smiled and nodded her approval.

"Okay," she said after she swallowed the

first mouthful. "What was your day like? You looked a little preoccupied when you got home."

I told her about my meeting with Raymond, his concerns, and the missing Sergeant Lake.

"Are you sure the sergeant is missing, and not just off somewhere with friends?"

"The way the woman next door described him, Rory Lake doesn't sound like the type to just go off without notifying someone," I said. As I said it, I realized that it had been nagging at me ever since I'd looked through the kitchen window. Lake was a career noncom with a bright future in the army. There was no way he'd risk it for a weekend toot. I didn't know what had happened to him, but I was determined to find out.

"Well, knowing you, you won't stop until you've found him and figured out what's going on," she said. "Do you think it has anything to do with this Armcor place?"

"Not really. Armcor might be shaving test results, or even outright lying, but this doesn't sound like something a company like that would do. No, there's something else going on here. I just can't figure out what it is."

But, she was right about one thing, though . . . I wouldn't rest until I did figure it out.

We finished dinner and drove back home, arriving around midnight. After a quick shower, we hopped in bed and played around for a while, but both of us were beat, so after a little kissing and fooling around, we rolled over and went to sleep.

# # #

The dream began as it always did. I was in a place filled with a mist. A formless place with dark, unrecognizable shapes intersperse throughout. There was no sound, no smells, and I couldn't see my feet. I could feel a spongy surface beneath them, though, and I was moving forward, causing the mist to part and then curl around me.

Time, and the sense of the passage of time – well, the only thing I can say is, it was distorted. I knew, for instance, that I'd only been asleep for a short while, but I was confused as to how long I'd been walking in this place. Before, when I had this dream, I didn't know where I was, nor did I know where I was going, only that I had somewhere to be – this time, I knew where I was going, even though I couldn't see my destination. This was different than previous dreams, and somehow unsettling.

Unsettling or not, I kept walking through the misty, formless void until the dark shapes resolved themselves into trees. I kept walking, and soft sounds began to fill the space that had until then been without sound. At first, there was the soft whisper of wind brushing the leaves and needles of the hardwoods and evergreens that surrounded me. Then . . . I heard the bubbling sound of water rushing over rocks. My destination was directly ahead.

As the sound of the rushing water grew

louder, the mist began to thin. I could see my feet as they brushed across the green carpet beneath me.

I reached the edge of the stream. I stood there, gazing across its width, knowing it I could not cross it, waiting . . . waiting.

And then, they appeared.

They came out of the haze on the other side of the stream, two figures that were so familiar. Sarah, petite, medium brown skin and flowing black hair, with smiling eyes, and Ethan, big for a six-year-old, almost half his mother's height, dark brown like me, but with his mother's silky black hair, he stood at her side, his face half hidden in the folds of her skirt.

They were as I last remembered them. Sarah was wearing a skirt that stopped just below her knees, and a blouse that accented her small, conical breasts. Ethan wore his soccer jersey and shorts, with knee length socks. I'd had to work a late shift at the Pentagon, so Sarah had driven Ethan and some of his team mates to a late evening soccer game in Arlington, Virginia. On the way back, driving northeast on Arlington Boulevard, the van Sarah was driving was T-boned by a truck driver who'd run a stop sign. I'd gotten home, and was waiting for them to arrive so we could go out for a quick supper, when the police arrived at the door to our brownstone house in the Georgetown University area to inform me of the accident.

The dreams began about a year later,

always when I faced a crisis or situation that bothered me. They'd become less frequent the past four or five years. In fact, I hadn't had the dream for a couple of years.

But, here I was, facing them across that damned stream that I couldn't cross, frustration creasing my face, while Ethan smiled shyly and Sarah gazed back at me with a benevolent look on her elfin face.

"Hello, Al my darling. It's been a long time." Her lips didn't move, but her musical voice was clear in my head.

Over the years I'd become accustomed to this method of communication, so I no longer muttered incoherently in my sleep.

"It's been too long," I thought back at her. *"I've missed you guys."*

They both frowned at me. Ethan looked old beyond his years, and wise.

"Don't you think it's time you let go and moved on?" Sarah's voice had a tinge of sadness in it.

"I suppose you're right, but it's just too hard to let go. I'm not sure I want to forget you"

"You won't forget us, I promise you that. We'll always be in your heart. But, you're in danger of allowing these dreams to become a crutch that, rather than helping you walk, could cripple you."

That was something that was familiar. In my dreams Sarah was always saying things that made no sense until I'd forgot about them for a while, and then days later I'd see the meaning.

"Talking to you in my dreams has helped me solve some pretty thorny problems. You're so much wiser than me."

She shook her head. Her hair swayed languidly, covering and uncovering her sparkling eyes.

"No, darling, I'm not wise, and I really haven't helped you solve your problems. The answers have always been in you, you've just failed to realize it. That's why you need to let go."

I felt that she was trying to tell me something, but I was missing the point again.

"I don't know if I can. It's not like I can control my dreams."

"You have more control than you realize." She smiled sadly again. *"I think you know that. You just need to accept it."*

I began to feel sad. It came on all of a sudden. I could feel the hot wetness of tears streaming down my cheeks.

"Are you saying this is the last time I'll see you two in my dreams?"

"I don't know, darling. Only time will tell . . . only time will tell . . . only time will . . .," as her voice faded from my mind, their images wavered and then faded from view, leaving me standing there on the banks of that stream listening to the bubbling of the water and feeling the water on my face.

# # #

I woke up lying on my back staring up at the ceiling as the first gray light of dawn slipped through a crack in the curtain. I felt for my face. It was slick and wet with tears.

5.

The rest of the weekend passed quietly. I remembered that I'd had a disturbing dream, but unlike past dreams, which I recalled vividly upon waking up, I couldn't remember the details of this one, only that it had made me very sad.

I got up at 5:00 Monday morning, rousted Sandra out of bed, and had her join me for my morning run through the forest behind the house. Afterwards we did thirty minutes on the heavy bag in the barn, and while she went in to shower I sat on the back porch and meditated for twenty minutes.

Sandra put on her makeup while I showered. That we finished at roughly the same time says more about how fast she does the makeup thing than how long it takes me to shower. My years in the army had taught me to get in, soap up, scrub, rinse, and dry in as short a time as possible. I'm the same with brushing the teeth and shaving, no wasted motions. As for Sandra, in the first place, she doesn't wear a lot of makeup, and in the second, what she does wear is minimal and applied as quickly as I slap on after shave.

We fixed breakfast together, me frying sausage and eggs and making coffee, her toasting bread and pouring grapefruit juice. We took our time eating. Afterwards I shooed her out of the house and off to school, and cleaned the kitchen before heading in to my place of business.

The office I share with my partner Heather is on Fourth Street in the District, and I get there by way of River Road, Cabin John Parkway and Canal Road to Whitehurst Freeway, past the Kennedy Center and around behind the Lincoln Memorial to Independence Avenue. From there it's an easy drive to Maine Avenue and on to the Waterfront area.

We're on the second floor of an old wood and brick building that looks like a roadside motel that's seen better days. Each tenant in the building has four parking spaces. Only one of ours was occupied; Heather's Honda was in its usual place. I parked next to her and went upstairs.

She was waiting at her desk, her notepad in hand when I walked in. She looked at her watch.

"I know I'm a little late," I said. "I had to

clean up before I left home."

She shrugged. "Okay, pull up a chair, and I'll fill you in on what I found out about Armcor."

I turned her visitor's chair around and straddled it. "Sure, but before you do, make a note of this . . . I went to Rory Lake's place Friday and his neighbor said he's been missing since the previous Friday. We need to try and track him down."

She made a note on a blank page of her notebook.

"Right, I'll get on it this morning," she said. "Now, to Armcor. Quite an outfit that one is."

Quite an outfit didn't really accurately describe Armcor. I'm not sure the language has appropriate words for an organization like Armcor.

Haydn Winchester, who had been a junior official in the Reagan administration, had founded the company after his boss left office. He'd parlayed his government connections to transform a seat of the pants operation into a multi-million dollar consulting and security firm that made most of its money providing security guards to government agencies and security escorts to corporate VIPs.

In 2000, Armcor had moved into providing security hardware, starting with small arms and personal body armor. Armcor had been one of about a dozen bidders on the contract to weaponized surveillance drones, and had surprised everyone by being selected as one of three companies to build prototypes. The company had no previous experience in unmanned vehicles or robotics, and there were rumors that someone in the Pentagon had intervened on Armcor's behalf. Staff Sergeant Rory Lake had been assigned as the project observer at Armcor, there to ensure the terms of the contract were complied with.

That brought us up to the current moment. She'd not been able to find out anything about Rory Lake's suspicions.

"So, we have a company with no experience building UAVs winning a contract to deliver weaponized UAVs to the government," I said. "Then, the government watchdog on the project suspects something's amiss and shortly thereafter he turns up missing. What we have here, my dear, is a first class mystery."

"You could put it that way," she said. "I'm trying to track down the source of the rumors of undue influence on the contract award. That won't be easy. Did your friend give you any details about how they were cooking the test results?"

"No, and frankly, I forgot to ask him."

She frowned at me. I felt chastened. I'd been her mentor in the PI business, and here she was reminding me that I'd made a dumb rookie mistake.

"Anything he can tell you would help," she said. "Now, about this Sergeant Lake . . . are you sure he didn't just take off somewhere?"

How was I to answer that question? I didn't

really know Lake. But, I knew his type, the career soldier with no family other than the army. He'd probably enlisted right out of high school. According to what Raymond had told me, he'd never married, hadn't even had a steady girlfriend as far as he knew. Guys like that don't go AWOL. There had to be another reason he was missing, but I was just missing it.

"I'm pretty sure he didn't," I said. Then, I had a thought. "What did you find out about this guy Winchester and any other individuals at Armcor, in particular those involved with the drone project?"

She flipped back to the front of her pad. "There was a lot on Winchester," she said. "As for the drone project, there were only two people in Armcor who seemed privy to what was going on with that . . . Winchester and a woman named Lila Thissen."

As usual, Heather had been thorough in her research. In a short time, she'd amassed a wealth of information on Winchester and Thissen.

A native of Salt Lake City, Utah, Winchester had come to Washington, DC in 1972 to attend Georgetown University. After getting his bachelor's degree in political science, he'd gone to work for an ultra-conservative member of the House of Representatives as a legislative aide. When Ronald Reagan was elected in 1980, Winchester's boss had used his influence with the cadre of conservatives surrounding the former California governor to get him an appointment to a junior position in the White House. Over the next eight years, he rose higher in the pecking order, and by the time Reagan left office in 1989, replaced by his vice president, George H.W. Bush, Winchester was an assistant secretary of defense dealing with procurement issues. Bush, somewhat less ideological than his predecessor, cleaned house, placing more moderate people in many of the appointed positions. Winchester, reading the writing on the wall, tendered his resignation, and, within six months, was CEO of the newly formed Armcor. He traded on his Pentagon and White House contacts to get low level contracts in the early years, but by 2000, the company's revenue had made him a very wealthy man. At 48, he was one of the wealthiest men in the Washington area, and as a generous donor to conservative political causes, one of the most influential according to Heather's research.

Lila Thissen, a 30-year-old Ohio native, was a unique individual. She was one of a hand full of women active in the defense consulting business, and the only one to head a major hardware program for a defense contractor. She had also graduated from Georgetown University – ten years after Winchester - earning a degree in international relations. When Winchester started Armcor, she'd been working for three years as a junior civil servant at the Defense Department. She'd been one of the first people he'd hired, and had risen through the ranks of Armcor until she was effectively his second in command.

"They sound like a couple of heavy hitters in the defense contracting world," I said when she'd finished telling me about them.

"They do wield a lot of influence in this town," she said. "More than you'd expect from a small company that came late to the game."

"That would lend credence to the rumors of insider influence in the contracts they've been awarded."

"But, they've covered their tracks well. I haven't been able to find anything but rumors – nothing concrete."

People believe that everything about everyone can be found on the Internet. That's not too far from the truth – but, it's not the whole truth. Sometimes, the most important facts about people are not committed to writing. The things that help you to truly understand people are often the content of conversations held behind closed doors, when no notes are taken. In particular, when people are doing things on the wrong side of the law, they're not likely to make a file.

If I was going to know what was going on at Armcor, I was going to have to do what I'd learned to do during Special Forces training – I was going to have to get eyes on target.

6.

I needed to get inside Armcor, so I called Bill Raymond to see if he could open any doors for me. I also told him about my visit to Rory Lake's house.

"That's worrying," he said. "Lake's not the type to go off without telling me. He's one of the most straight laced noncoms I know."

"I figured as much. Look, I need to get inside Armcor."

"You don't think they might have done anything to him, do you?" There was worry in his voice that came over the line clearly.

"I can't say for sure," I said. "I need to do some on-site checking before I'm certain."

He was silent for a long time. When he spoke, his voice was tense. "It won't be easy. Defense contractors have tighter security sometimes than we do here in the five-sided puzzle palace. How much of your army protocol do you remember?"

"Depends on what I have to do and who

I'd have to fool."

"You think you could pretend to be a Department of the Army civilian?"

"I'm no technician," I said. "I can barely get my computer working without my partner's help."

"I was thinking more bureaucrat than technician." He laughed. "If Lake's missing, it means he probably hasn't shown up at the contractor's site. You think you could pull off being a green eyeshade's type trying to find out where's he gotten to?"

I thought about that for a few seconds. Hell, I might just be able to pull it off. It was close enough to the truth – I was trying to figure out where Lake was. I figured I could play the part of an officious minor bureaucrat. Not that I had any experience being one, but I'd suffered at the hands of more than one. "Sure, I can do that."

"It's probably best if you use your real name," he said. He then gave me Armcor's address – on King Street in Alexandria – and some more information about the drone project and Sergeant Lake. "Since you're just a paper pusher," he continued. "You shouldn't need any ID beyond your driver's license. Hopefully they won't ask to see a Pentagon badge."

"If they do, I'll just say I left it at home. Listen, if you hear from Lake, let me know right away."

"Al, do you want me to go with you to

Armcor?"

"I appreciate the offer," I said. "But, if you're there I'd have no excuse to pry. I'll let you know what I find. Look, don't worry. From what you told me about Lake, he can take care of himself."

As I said it, I realized that I too was beginning to worry about the young sergeant. I hoped I was right about his ability to take care of himself.

Charles Ray

7.

The first thing he noticed was the tickling sensation of dust in his nostrils. He fought back the urge to sneeze. Next, as he blinked his eyes, he noticed the darkness . . . then he felt the pressure of the rough cloth on his face. He strained forward, and felt the bands around his chest and arms. He heard the scraping and thumping sounds of wood on wood.

He was having trouble concentrating. At first, he couldn't remember who he was. Slowly, achingly slow in fact, that knowledge emerged from somewhere in his befogged brain.

Rory Alan Lake, Staff Sergeant, U.S. Army, Social Security Number 427-66-5555.

Now, why would I think that? Am I a prisoner of war? No, wait, that's not right. I wasn't in a war zone. I was assigned desk duty – at the Pentagon? No, I was a . . . it had something to do with procurement.

Colonel William Raymond . . . I work for Colonel Raymond. I . . . I spoke to him. When? What time is it? What day is it? Where the fuck am I?

He could feel the darkness closing in about his head, and the first hint of panic set in.

No, dammit. Remember your training. Focus . . . breathe . . . get it under control!

He slowed his breathing, calming his mind. As his heartbeat dropped close to normal, his other senses sharpened. Swiveling his head slowly, he realized that there was some kind of cloth over his head. It felt rough, probably muslin or burlap, the kind of thing the instructors had used during interrogation training at Bragg. Tensing his arm muscles, he got the feel of his bindings. Small cord or rope, tied tightly. No room to wiggle and loosen it. He could also feel the cords at his ankles.

He was tied to some kind of wooden, straight back chair. The surface under his feet felt like concrete. He could hear a humming sound, like a fan – a furnace fan – echoing off brick or concrete. That and the dust in the air led to the conclusion that he was probably in a basement somewhere.

How the hell did I get here? His memory was still fuzzy. He remembered coming home from . . . Armcor . . . his duty station was Armcor, in a building in Alexandria . . . on King Street. It was Colonel Raymond who worked at the Pentagon, and he'd reported a problem to him. Armcor's executives were faking test results for their drone, Loki. It couldn't do what they were claiming . . . or it had some kind of flaw that would cause it not to work properly . . . he couldn't remember clearly what, he just knew that the colonel needed to know. Raymond had told him he'd take care of it. The colonel was a straight shooter. Better than many of the officers Lake had worked with since enlisting straight out of high school. He'd scored higher on the entrance exams than anyone else in his small South Texas town, and had out-performed everyone in his basic training battalion. The battalion commander had recommended that he apply for Officer Candidate School, but Lake hadn't been impressed with some of the OCS officers who worked as training officers – he hadn't been impressed with most of the officers in fact, so he'd turned it down. The battalion commander had been disappointed. He'd told Lake that the army was looking to commission more blacks, and that he was a fool for turning down the chance to be an officer. Lake then realized that the man was just trying to fill an equal opportunity quota, so he'd been glad he'd turned him down. Most of the officers he'd worked with as he climbed up the enlisted ranks had been white, most had been so-so. But, Raymond had been different. The man truly seemed not to notice things like race and gender, and he only seemed to care how well a soldier did the job. He was the first officer Lake had truly respected.

The colonel will come through. Now, I just have to survive until he finds me.

In order to do that, though, he'd have to figure out where he was, and who was holding him and why. He strained to remember.

Slowly the fog cleared. He'd gone home Friday. He remembered saying hello to his neighbor, Lorraine Zeller. Old Ms. Zeller was a nosey one, but basically harmless, and she seemed to enjoy it when he talked to her. He'd then gone inside and made supper, but he hadn't been too hungry, so he'd left it half eaten on the counter near the kitchen sink, planning to eat it later.

He didn't feel like sleeping, so he'd sat in the living room watching TV until around ten when . . . Morgan came over. Morgan Freer, a bear of a white man who'd struck up a conversation with him in a bar down Route 1 about six months earlier, and who also seemed to like his company. He'd come over and suggested they hit a few of the bars in Georgetown, maybe pick up some college chicks. He'd been bored, and even though he wasn't in the mood, he'd agreed.

They ended up at a hole in the wall bar

off Wisconsin Avenue near P Street. It had been crowded with students from Georgetown and the kind of people who hang around such places looking for a student with a fat wallet and a thirst for alcohol. They took a table in a corner near the back, and ordered drinks – whiskey and soda. From that point things got fuzzy, and try as he might, he couldn't remember what happened after he took that first drink.

His throat felt dry and raspy, and he had a slight headache and ringing in his ears.

How many drinks did I have? He cleared his throat. *Man, I could really use a drink of water.* "Hey," he called. "Anyone here? Could I get some water?"

All he heard, other than the sound of his own voice, muffled by whatever was over his head, was the steady drone of the fan that was somewhere nearby.

"Why do you have me here," he said in a louder voice. "Come on, let me the hell out of here."

Then, he waited, his senses probing his surroundings. It seemed like an eternity until he noticed a subtle change – a shift in the air, or the whisper of shoes on the concrete floor. He wasn't alone.

"Who's there? Come on, tell me who you are and why you have me here, please."

The whisper of footsteps came closer. Then, he could feel the presence of a body near his, and smell a faint odor of stale liquor and the minty aroma of after shave – an odor he finally recognized. He knew who his captor was.

"Hello, Rory," a familiar voice said. "Glad you're finally awake. You and I have some business to discuss."

8.

I had an important stop to make before visiting Armcor. I drove back out to Montgomery County, west on River Road, almost to the little town of Poolesville, then north on an unmarked dirt road that ended at a large log cabin. My old friend, Carlton 'Blood' Raine, a retired CIA agent, was, as usual, waiting for me on the front porch.

I know he had sensors planted in the trees along the road leading up to his house, but try as I might I'd never been able to spot them. He had, though, let me see the video monitors he kept in the strong room behind the living room. With the devices he got from his former colleagues at Langley, he could watch visitors from the moment they turned off River Road. Anyone trying to sneak up on him was in for a surprise. The foliage around his house had been cut back in a large one-hundred yard circle, and he had enough weaponry in his strong room to hold off a regiment.

"Hello, young fellow," he said, as I got out of the car. "To what do I owe the pleasure of your visit this early on a work day?"

We shook hands. For a man in his eighties, his grip was strong.

"I'm working on a case, and I need your expert advice on it," I said.

"Well, come on in. I just made a fresh pot of coffee . . . Jamaican, the kind you like. Elizabeth's off at some meeting in Atlanta until the weekend, so I'm just rattling around here by myself."

I followed him in. We walked through the living room to the strong room, behind the metal reinforced door. Across the back wall was a work bench with a space-age looking control panel in front of a high-backed captain's chair. On the shelf in front of the chair were four color monitors, each showing a different view of the outside of the cabin. A silver coffee urn sat next to the control panel. Next to the urn were four large coffee mugs. He poured one for me, and topped off another. I took a sip. It was primo Jamaican, brewed just so. He motioned me to a chair next to his, not quite as big or imposing as his captain's chair, but comfortable.

"Okay, son," he said, after we were seated. "What can I tell you?"

"What can you tell me about a company

called Armcor?"

His bushy gray eyebrows arched upwards. "Armcor, eh? How'd they get on your radar?"

I gave him a quick background on the case. When I'd finished, he shook his head.

"I've heard things about Haydn Winchester *and* Lila Thissen," he said. "But, kidnapping doesn't fit their profile. They'd be more likely to dig up dirt on their enemies and threaten to smear them."

"Yeah, but Lake is missing, and he doesn't strike me as the type to go over the hill."

"Let's say you're right about that, are you sure him being missing has anything to do with Armcor, and not something else. Maybe he got cross ways with some gal's husband."

I hadn't considered that. Lake was single, so that was possible, but my gut told me it wasn't probable.

"I just don't know," I said. "I'll have to work on that. If you're right about Winchester and Thissen, though, I might just be working two cases here. Which brings me to the real reason I came to see you. I'm going to Armcor today. You got any suggestions for me on how to deal with them?"

He drained his cup, and took his time refilling it. After taking a sip, he put the cup down and turned to face me. "Well, I think you're using the right cover," he said. "Keep it simple, and there's less chance of blowing it.

Problem for you is going to be acting like a bureaucrat." He laughed. "You know you're not exactly the bureaucratic type."

"I figure I'll just act self-important, and ask a lot of dumb ass questions, and they'll never know the difference."

"Okay, I think you'll do well," he said. "But, you'll have to do better than that if you want to find out if they're up to shenanigans."

He then explained how the place was likely set up, with test labs and outside test areas secured from prying eyes – not enemy agents, but competitors. What I'd need to try and get a look at was the test documents, which would probably be in an area even more secure than the labs, and accessible by only a few people.

A snap – just waltz into a highly secure facility, find documents showing the owners were defrauding the government and either steal them or get photos of them. Oh yeah, a cake walk. Just in case I decided to try and get covert photos, he let me borrow one of the gadgets he got occasionally from his friends to test; a miniature camera that looked like one of those disposable lighters. It even had a reservoir for lighter fuel, a wick and a flint. In other words, it worked as a lighter. It was digital, recording high resolution images on a chip concealed in the base. Along with the camera, he gave me a connector that would allow me to upload the images to a computer.

I slipped the device into my pocket, thanked him, and left.

Charles Ray

9.

Before leaving Raine's house, I called Bill Raymond to have him alert Armcor that I was on my way. I drove to Alexandria by way of the I-495 Beltway off River Road and the George Washington Memorial Parkway. It was just after ten in the morning so, while the beltway was crowded as usual with trucks, vans, pickups, and cars all jockeying to be 'in front' of everyone else, the parkway was nearly empty. At Arlington National Cemetery I got on Virginia Route 110 which turns into US Highway 1 as it passes the Pentagon and enters the city of Alexandria. Once it enters Alexandria, especially the Old Town historic district, it becomes a crowded two-way street with a traffic light at almost every intersection. I turned right on King Street at the southern end of Old Town and drove the remaining twenty blocks to Armcor.

It was pretty much as Raine had said it would be – an ultra-modern building, far larger than it needed to be, and separated from all the buildings around it. A six-story building with clean lines and covered in glass all around the ground floor, it was surrounded by a large swath of close-cropped lawn. A separate building, separated from the main building by a fifty yard long covered walkway, served as a two-story parking garage. Drivers had to stop at the entrance to the garage and identify themselves to a camera-mike device set at car window level. If you were on the visitors list, the gate raised to allow you to enter and park.

There were a number of cars parked on the ground level, but I was able to find a space large enough for the Volkswagen just before the ramp to the second level. As I made my way to the walkway, I noticed video surveillance cameras placed strategically so that the entire level was covered. I imagined that someone was sitting in a darkened room staring at me on a video screen. As I approached the end of the walkway, I also noticed that the glass around the ground floor of the main building was tinted. I couldn't see inside the building – only my reflection as I approached.

The entrance doors swung inward as I neared them. I was impressed. Armcor seemed to have a top of the line security set up.

The entrance lobby was large, taking up what appeared to be the front half of the building. Through the floor to ceiling glass walls I also had a clear view of the exterior. Across from the entrance was a chest-high metal desk behind which sat four uniformed security guards. A broad shouldered man with close-cropped brown hair and a no-nonsense look stood in front of the desk. He wore a plain blue suit that was well tailored, but failed to conceal the bulge of a weapon under his left arm. He stepped away from the desk and met me halfway across the lobby.

"You're Mr. Pennyback from Colonel Raymond's office," he said. "I'm Alec Sweeney, chief of security. Could I see some ID?"

Raine had prepared me for this. I reached into my shirt pocket, and then wrinkled my brow in confusion. "Damn," I said. "Colonel Raymond called me at home and told me to come here. I left my Pentagon pass on my dresser. Would my driver's license do?"

He frowned at me. "Yeah, I guess so. The Colonel described you, so as long as your license photo matches, you're good to go."

I took my Maryland driver's license from my wallet and handed it to him. He scrutinized it closely, holding it up so he could look at the photo and my face at the same time. Then, he nodded and handed it back.

"Okay, you're good," he said. "Now, what is it you want here? Raymond didn't give me any details other than it had to do with

Sergeant Lake."

This was the crucial moment. If I could convince him of my bona fides now, I was close to home free. "Sergeant Lake failed to check in on September 19 as scheduled, and right now his whereabouts are unknown. Before the colonel boots it up the chain of command, he wanted me to check to see if anyone here's been in touch with him."

His brow wrinkled and his eyes narrowed. "Now that you mention it, the Friday before that is the last time he was here. I figured you guys had just sent him off somewhere else. Okay, what do you want to do?"

"I suppose I should start with talking to the people he worked with here," I said. "And then, maybe if I could take a look at whatever space you guys gave him as an office?"

"Well, if you want to talk to the person he dealt with most, that would be Ms. Thissen." He pronounced it 'Thigh-son.' "I'll take you up to her office."

I followed him around the security desk. I hadn't noticed the bank of elevators in the back wall, just to the left of the security desk. Except for the floor indicator panel above them, and the discrete call buttons to each side, they were almost invisible. They were quiet too. The door slid soundlessly open as soon as he thumbed the button. He stood aside to let me enter, and the followed. Once inside, he took a plastic key card from his pocket and slipped it into a slot, and then punched the button for the sixth floor. The doors closed and the car rose silently, but rapidly.

I never felt the elevator stop, but the doors slid open, and again Sweeney stood aside to let me go first. I stepped out and into a wide open space half as big as the lobby. An overly made up blonde with lots of cleavage showing sat behind a large glass top desk containing a computer screen and a large keyboard and nothing else sat directly in front of the elevator, about ten steps away. Behind her and to either side were two unmarked doors. To the right and left, from floor to ceiling the wall was glass with a dizzying view of the world outside. The blonde looked up and smiled as Sweeney and I took the ten steps to her desk.

"Good morning, Alec," the blonde said brightly. "This must be Mr. Pennyback. Is he here to see Mr. Winchester or Ms. Thissen?"

Armcor certainly shared information better than most of the government bureaucracies I know.

"Morning, Felicity," Sweeney said. "Yeah, this is Mr. Pennyback, and he'd like to talk to Ms. Thissen."

"Just a moment, I'll see if she's available." She punched some keys on the keyboard, and after a second looked at the screen. "Yes, she's available. You can go right in, Mr. Pennyback." She motioned to the door on her left.

"Call me when he's done, Felicity," Sweeney said. "And, I'll come up and escort him out." He turned and proffered his hand. "This is Felicity Lyon, Mr. Pennyback. She'll take care of you as long as you're here on the sixth floor. I'll see you when you're done talking to Ms. Thissen."

He turned and left. I went to the door Felicity Lyon had indicated, pushed it open, and entered.

Lila Thissen's office was . . . opulent. The walls on the right and left were floor to ceiling shelves containing rare books, trophies, diplomas and certificates clearly intended to impress visitors – and working. Thissen sat behind a large mahogany desk. On it were a laptop computer, a push button phone, and a gold pen set. No inbox or outbox, and nary a piece of paper in sight. The wall behind her was glass with a view of Alexandria spread out below.

If Hollywood was looking to cast someone in the role of a beautiful, but hard looking woman executive, they'd probably hire Lila Thissen to play herself. She was beautiful in a classical way, with pale skin that the old writers described as alabaster, light brown hair pulled back severely and done up in a precise bun at the back, and light blue eyes that had about as much warmth as a python. The beige suit jacket she wore clung to medium sized, but shapely breasts, and as she stood to greet me, I could see that the matching skirt hugged curves that would have looked good in a bikini. She extended her hand. Her grip was firm and warm.

"Mr. Pennyback, Colonel Raymond said you'd probably want to talk to me about Sergeant Lake," she said in a brisk 'let's get down to business tone.' "What precisely do you wish to know?"

She motioned toward a chair at the left side of her desk and sat back down herself, turning her chair to face me and crossing shapely legs.

"Thanks for seeing me, Ms. Thissen," I said. "The colonel wanted me to inquire about Sergeant Lake because we haven't heard from him since September 14. He didn't check in on the nineteenth as he was supposed to do."

She turned her laptop so I couldn't see the screen, and typed on the keyboard.

"Yes," she said, looking back at me. "That was the last time I met with him as well. We spoke on Friday the fifteenth just before noon. I haven't seen him since."

"Didn't you think it strange that he'd not show up for work for such an extended period of time?"

"Mr. Pennyback, nothing the military does strikes me as strange anymore." She laughed ruefully. "Since September 11, this whole town's been paranoid. I just figured he'd been reassigned to some other duty and they hadn't gotten around to informing us."

She said it with an even voice, and it

made sense, because the military did have a tendency sometimes to ignore civilians, but the way she refused to make eye contact as she spoke told me she was either lying or at a minimum holding something back.

There was nothing to be gained, however, from confronting her at this point. I needed more ammunition.

"Did Sergeant Lake have any problems here that you're aware of?"

"I don't understand. What kind of problems would he have here?"

Typical reaction to someone who is planning to lie – answer a question with a question.

"I mean related to the work," I said. "Were there any problems with the project he was monitoring?"

Her eyebrows twitched, and she briefly looked down at her knee. "No, not at all," she said. "The project is going according to schedule. Sergeant Lake got along with everyone working on the project . . . in fact he got along well with everyone here at Armcor."

More lies. This time, there was a slight hitch in her voice. It might not have been noticed by the average person, but I picked up on it.

"I see. Well, I'd like to take a look at his work space."

This time, her eyebrow twitch was noticeable. I would have been able to see it from across the room.

"I don't know if that's possible," she said. "He had access to proprietary information."

I fixed her with what I thought was my best bureaucratic look – total indifference leavened with a bit of arrogant superiority. "I'm well aware of that, Ms. Thissen," I said. "Might I remind you, though, that it is *my* agency that is paying your company to develop this project, so ultimately *we* are the owners of that information. In addition, since Sergeant Lake is assigned to our office, anything he creates belongs to us."

Her eyes widened a fraction – just a bit of shock I suppose at being talked to in that tone – and her pupils dilated. Raymond, at my request, had been purposely vague about my position within his office. That would leave doubt as to the level of influence I had over the contract. I could see from her expression that it had the desired effect.

"Well . . . of course," she said. "I'm aware of that . . . sure, you can see Lake's office. It's on the floor below us. I'll call Alec to come up and escort you." She reached for the phone, but her hand stopped a few inches from it and her gaze drifted to a point to my right and behind me.

"It might be best if you escorted Mr. Pennyback, Lila," a deep male voice from behind me said. "He might have questions that Alec can't answer."

I turned to see a man about my height, but of lighter build, wearing gray pants and a vest over a light blue silk shirt with a red 'power' tie, standing in the doorway. I recognized Haydn Winchester from the photo Heather had found of him on the Internet. Her research indicated that he was two years older than my fifty, but he looked a decade older, with a sallow complexion, deep set blue eyes with bags under them, and stringy brown hair that had receded to the top of his narrow skull. His gaze drifted over me as if I was of no consequence and speared into Thissen. She stared back, and then, like a dog in a pack that has been challenged by the alpha male leader, let her gaze drop in submission.

"Of course, Haydn," she said. "That's a good idea. Mr. Pennyback, this is our CEO, Haydn Winchester."

I stood as he walked toward me, his hand extended. I took his hand. His grip was firm, and his eyes bored into mine as we shook.

"Pleased to meet you, Mr. Pennyback," he said. "I understand you're concerned about Sergeant Lake. A good man, Lake, I hope he's not in any kind of trouble."

"It's too early to speculate," I said. "Right now I'm just trying to get a sense of what's going on. How well did you know the sergeant?"

He looked at Thissen before responding to my question. Some unspoken communication passed between them. "Not very well," he said. "I think I only spoke to him two or three times, and never at any length. He worked primarily with Lila and her people."

"Primarily with me," Thissen said quickly. "He would observe the guys in the lab, but I don't think he ever really engaged with them."

"But, wasn't he supposed to be evaluating the technical specifications of . . . what do you call it . . . Loki?"

"Loki, that's correct," she said. "Named for the Norse god of trickery, and, yes, it was his job to ensure that we were meeting the technical requirements of the contract. But, he got his information from me. The engineers submitted their results to me, and I passed that information on to Sergeant Lake."

I don't know a lot about government contracting, but that sounded like a strange lash up to me. If Lake was supposed to be monitoring performance on the contract, it would seem more effective for him to get information directly from the people doing the work, instead of having it funneled through someone who could censor or edit it. Something about the way she said it, too, made me wonder if that was really the way he got his information.

"So, if there were technical problems, say something on the prototype wasn't working properly, he'd discuss it with you?"

She hesitated a fraction of a second too long before answering. "Of course he would."

"But, Ms. Thissen," I said. "If I understand correctly, you're not an engineer. How would you handle technical questions?"

"If something came up that was too technical for me," she said, blinking rapidly. "I would of course have an engineer in to explain it. But, that's academic, because nothing ever did in our conversations. The prototype works the way it's supposed to. The only problems we ever had were involving delivery times, and on one or two occasions the cost of components, but these were all eventually resolved."

I was convinced that she was blowing smoke at me. It was also interesting that Winchester stood there, silently observing. If someone was in my office, casting even vague aspersions on my pet project, I'd have something to say. He seemed content, though, to let Thissen carry the ball. At that moment, though, there was nothing I could do about it without blowing my cover.

"I see. Okay, can we go down to his office now?"

She stood. "Of course. Haydn, are you coming with us?"

"No," he said. "I just wanted to stick my head in and say hello. I'm sure you can answer whatever questions Mr. Pennyback might have." He stuck his hand out again. "Nice meeting you, Mr. Pennyback."

After a brief shake, he turned and left. Thissen brushed past me and headed for the door. A faint whiff of perfume tickled my nose as she passed. I followed, watching the sway of her hips appreciatively. From behind the hardness of her expression wasn't there to spoil the view.

She went to another almost invisible door, off to the side of the elevators, and slipped a plastic card into a slot in the wall. The door clicked, and she pulled it open, holding it for me to enter the stairwell. We went down one flight, and she pushed a door open. We entered a narrow hallway with the elevators on one side and doors on the other. She walked past four doors, opened the fifth, and entered, flipping on the light switch as she did.

10.

Staff Sergeant Rory Lake's office might have been sumptuous compared to anything he'd ever had in the army, but compared to Thissen's office it was a small broom closet.

A gray metal desk sat in the center of a windowless square. Behind the desk was a small swivel chair, comfortable, but hardly fancy. A credenza was behind the desk, and on top of it were Lake's trophies and mementos of the units he'd served in. Three-shelf bookcases sat to the right and left.

Thissen stood just inside the door and watched as I walked around, taking in the place.

The bookshelves held army technical and field manuals and several binders with the Armcor name and logo and long strings of numbers and technical terms. I picked one up and showed it to Thissen. "I take it this is a manual on the project?"

"Yes," she said. "If I remember correctly,

that particular one contains the component specifications."

I flipped through it. It contained page after page of cutaway drawings, photographs, charts, and columns of numbers that meant absolutely nothing to me. I didn't see anything that I recognized, so I put the binder back on the shelf. As I did, I noticed a small crossword puzzle magazine of the kind the post exchanges sell. It was wedged between two of the manuals, which struck me as strange. I eased it out and flipped it open. As I flipped through it, I noticed that most of the puzzles had been completed. I wondered why Lake would hang onto a magazine when he'd done the puzzles. Looking closer, though, I noticed that most of the answers were wrong. The words weren't even close to the clues, even the easy ones. As I looked at one of the puzzles a little closer, it hit me – if you read every other word across it made a sentence, *Loki test today failed. Report submitted indicates test successful.*

I took a slow, deep breath and slowly looked around at Thissen. She stood by the door not paying me any particular attention, probably bored at having to serve as my escort. I turned back and carefully slipped the magazine inside my shirt, and picked up another binder and held it up for her to see. "What is this one?"

She walked closer and peered down at the

spine. "That one is the required flight characteristics of Loki," she said. "I think it also includes the targeting requirements."

Along with drawings and photos, some of the prototype that I recognized, this one also had maps and isometric charts which were, like the component report, incomprehensible. I flipped through the binder slowly, stopping and studying charts every few pages in order to maintain my cover. When her attention drifted away, I put the binder back and moved to the credenza.

I studied the certificates and photos on top. Mostly photos of Lake with various high ranking officers, and a few of him with other GIs. The certificates were for the various schools and training courses he'd attended. He was a well-educated soldier. And, smart too. I imagine that when Armcor suspected he knew they were faking test results, they searched his office looking for evidence that he'd reported on them, and came up dry. He'd hidden his notes in plain sight like Poe's Purloined Letter. If I wasn't such a nosy type, I too might have missed them.

I was pretty sure Raymond would be able to use the notes in the crossword book to move against Armcor. Now, I had to find Lake.

Problem was I didn't have a clue where to start looking.

Charles Ray

11.

I thanked Thissen for her assistance and then went with her back to the sixth floor to wait for Sweeney to escort me back to the lobby. I felt eyes on me as I walked back to the parking garage, and figured cameras tracked my car until there were buildings between me and Armcor.

When I got to Route 1 in Old Town, I pulled over and called Raymond's cell phone.

He answered quietly, but didn't use my name.

"We need to meet," I said. "I just left Armcor, and I have information that Lake recorded about the faked test reports."

"Okay," he said after a pause. "It's almost lunch time. How far are you from Crystal City?"

"Just a few minutes. There's an Italian restaurant on Eads Street, *Luigi's*, how about meeting me there."

"Yeah, I know it. I'll be there in twenty

minutes," he said and rang off.

I found parking down the street from the place, put two dollars in the parking meter and walked back. It was 12:20, and it was crowded, but the waitress found a table for two near the bar. She put two menus on the table. I ordered an iced tea and told her I'd order when my guest arrived. She quickly brought the tea and went back to taking care of her other tables.

Raymond arrived ten minutes after me. He waved as he saw me and walked over, followed immediately by the waitress.

"What would you like?" I asked as I shook his hand. "I was thinking about spaghetti and meatballs with garlic bread myself."

He looked up at the waitress. "Sounds good to me, make it two, and I'll have iced tea as well."

When she'd gone, he turned his attention to me. "You said you had something Lake wrote about Armcor faking test results?"

I took the magazine from my shirt, opened it and put it on the table. I showed him the way Lake had inserted his reports in the puzzles. After reading the first three, he sat back and whistled.

"Yeah," I said. "Looks like Armcor's been stringing you guys along from the get go."

"Where'd you find this?"

"It was in his office, right in plain sight."

"I'm not surprised," he said. "Lake's one

smart cookie. By the way, do you have a line on where he is?"

I shook my head. "His neighbor said he left his house around midnight with a big white guy who's been there a few times. I'll let you take care of Armcor. I'll get right on trying to track him down."

"How do you plan to do that?"

"I wish I knew." I shrugged. "I'll come up with something." I usually do. I just hoped this wouldn't be the first time I didn't.

Charles Ray

12.

Raymond took the magazine back with him to the Pentagon, and I drove back to my office.

"Okay, Heather, we've got to pull out all the stops to find Sergeant Lake," I said as I walked through the door. "I have a bad feeling about his disappearance."

She looked up at me, frowning and making cute little wrinkles in her forehead. "It would help if I had some starting point . . . what are we trying to determine?"

Now, my own brow wrinkled. What were we trying to find out? An idea popped into my mind. It was a long shot, but it was better than nothing.

"His neighbor said he left his house late with another guy," I said. "Sounds like maybe a drinking buddy. Maybe if we could figure out where he hung out, we could get a line on our mystery man."

"That's as good a place as any to start," she said. She laid a well-manicured finger against her nose. "I have an idea. He probably doesn't carry a lot of cash with him when he goes out, so maybe we can figure out his movements by his credit card charges. I have a friend at Metro Police who might be able to run a quick check for me."

I didn't ask who the friend was, or how she'd manage to get the job done. Heather has her methods, and I think sometimes it's best that I not know any more about them than I already do.

"Okay, get on that," I said. "I need to do some serious thinking." Meaning, I needed to sit in the quiet of my office and meditate to determine my next step, which was just as well, because she didn't really like having me hanging over her shoulder while she worked her information retrieval magic.

She just nodded, already turning to her computer. I went into my office and shut the door.

I have this relatively small space containing a desk that I bought at a military surplus auction, a scuffed leather executive chair that I got for a steal at the same auction, two book cases containing phone books, and investigative information pamphlets, a few hunting prints on the walls alongside an autographed color photo of me with General Colin Powell when he was chairman of the Joint Chiefs of Staff and I was a young lieutenant colonel assigned to the Pentagon. On my desk, I have a laptop computer, which replaced the clunky desktop computer I once had, thanks to Heather's insistence that we upgrade our information technology. I keep note pads and extra pens in the desk, because even with the computer, I'm still more comfortable making notes on paper.

I sat behind my desk, leaned back in my chair, and stared at the ceiling, counting the fly specks and tiny cracks in the paint. To most people that might not seem like work, but believe me, in my business it's the hardest part . . . getting your mind around the problem and deciding which of a multitude of possible paths to follow.

I did a review of the case so far. Sergeant Lake, assigned to look over the shoulders of the people at Armcor, had uncovered problems and reported them to his boss, Colonel Raymond. Raymond had been unable to convince his boss, General Bennington to do anything about Lake's report. While the cryptic notes in the crossword puzzle magazines in Lake's office weren't conclusive proof of his allegations they were, along with Lila Thissen's evasiveness, enough to convince me that they were credible. It remained to be seen whether Raymond's boss would be convinced.

Lake's disappearance was another problem, which might or might not be related to the problem at Armcor. The key to that was identifying and locating the mystery man. Of that I was at least certain.

I sat up and retrieved a note pad and pen from my desk. I opened the pad to the first page and began making notes.

> **Armcor cooking test results**
> **Lake becomes aware and reports to his boss**
> **Armcor exec lying**
>
> **Lake goes missing**
> **Mystery man at his house – who is he?**
>
> **Could Armcor be involved in Lake going missing??**

I put the two question marks after the last question because there was nothing so far to tie Armcor to the mystery man, and while I sensed that Thissen was evasive about the Loki tests, I didn't really get a sense that she knew Lake's whereabouts. For now, I would continue to treat this as two separate cases.

It wasn't much to go on, but it was all I had, and until Heather came up with some places for me to look, I knew *what* I was hunting, but had no idea *where* to start hunting.

I pushed the pad aside and flipped up the lid of my computer. I pushed the little button to boot it up and sat there watching as the tiny – compared to my old computer – screen began to flicker. For its size it was powerful, and much faster than my old computer. In a few seconds I was rewarded with a nice colorful screen containing three little pictures, that Heather called icons, grouped on the left side. One was a stylized envelope, which was my email; another was a spiral coil for the Internet; and the third was a cartoon chess piece. I grabbed the mouse and moved it around until the little arrowhead pointer was centered over the chess piece, and then pressed the 'head' of the mouse.

I was quickly rewarded with a red and black chess board with white and black chess pieces in the proper positions for the beginning of a game. At the bottom of the screen, must beneath the board, was a little white square that blinked, indicating that I should select whether I wanted to play 'white' or 'black.' If I chose 'white' I got the first move, otherwise the computer moved first.

I chose 'white.' Moving the pieces was simple. I placed the pointer over the piece I wanted to move, clicked on it, then moved the pointer to the square to which I wanted to move and clicked on it. I decided to go with the classic Ruy Lopez opening, Pawn to Queen 4, which the computer countered with by moving the black Pawn to Queen 5, and we were off to the races. The game went twenty moves before the computer mated my King with a combined Knight-Rook fork check from which I had no escape.

Heather's tapping on my door just before she opened it saved me from the indignity of another loss. I logged out of the game and turned the computer off, closing the top cover before it had finished clearing the screen.

"You look like you have something," I said, smiling up at her.

She pulled my guest chair around and put her note pad on my desk.

"My friend at Metro came through." She opened the pad and showed me several lines of her precise handwriting. "I had her run Lake's credit charges for the past sixty days, just focusing on restaurants, clubs, and bars, and this is what she found."

There were two pages of charges at ten different establishments. Most were one-time charges for food, but two establishments showed multiple visits: five visits to *Jerry's Bar and Grill* on Highway 1 not far from Woodlawn, and six to *The Hotspot* on Lee Highway in Falls Church. My guess was that if he hung out with anyone it would be at a place he'd been to more than once, more than likely a bar or lounge, so I decided to pay a visit to these two first. Most of the charges were prior to September 11, but half of the visits to both these places had been during the week of September 10. The last charge at *Jerry's*, in fact, had been September 14.

I asked Heather to contact Raymond to have him fax us a recent photo of Lake, which he did right away. The photo was black and white, showing Lake in his dress uniform without headgear, but sharp enough that anyone having met him should be able to recognize him.

"Okay, Heather," I said after she gave me a copy of the photo. "I'm going home to get an early supper, and then I'll hit these two places tonight to see what I can find out. You keep digging to see if you can come up with anything else that might help us identify Lake's mystery friend."

Charles Ray

13.

Sandra and I had an early supper of tuna sandwiches and cream of crab soup, and spent an hour or so listening to classical music on NPR. I asked her if she wanted to accompany me on my information hunt, and with a wry smile that she'd rather hit the rack early, so at 8:30, I kissed her on the forehead, pulled on a light jacket, folded the photo of Lake and put it in the pocket, and headed for my first stop, *The Hotspot* in Falls Church.

I took George Washington Memorial Parkway to Rosslyn where I got on I-66 to the US 29/Lee Highway exit in Falls Church. *The Hotspot* was a trendy drinking establishment for young government employees who lived in or near Falls Church. A one-story, dimly lit, and overly crowded space; it shared a cramped mini-mall with a Denny's, a Starbucks, and two fashion boutiques. The tiny parking lot of the mall was filled, but fortunately I was able to find an empty slot on the street about a block past it. The evening was pleasant, and the sidewalks were populated by couples out for the evening.

There were no empty tables in the place, and I had to wedge myself between two buxom young ladies at the bar. "Sorry if I'm intruding on your conversation," I said. "I just need to ask the bartender a question."

The one on my left, a redhead with a jewel stud in her left nostril, smiled up at me. "We're not together," she said. "And, you can stay as long as you want."

Seeing that the redhead had already apparently made her move, the brunette on my right just smiled and turned her attention back to her drink.

The bartender, a young guy who looked like he was barely old enough to be out of high school, but who was probably a college student, was at the far end of the bar. I signaled him with my left hand, and with my right withdrew the picture of Lake from my jacket and spread it out on the bar.

"Hey," the blonde said, jostling my arm. "I know him." She put a long, red-lacquered fingernail on Lake's face. "He bought me drinks a couple weeks ago."

She had my interest now. "Was he with someone at the time?"

"Come on now, you think a guy in here with girl is going to buy another girl a drink?" She laughed.

"I mean, was he with another guy?" She was good looking, but not too bright.

"Oh," she said. "No, he was alone. Standing right about where you are in fact."

The bartender leaned forward. "Can I get you anything, buddy?"

I put a finger on the picture. "Yeah, information," I said. "You recognize this guy?"

He picked the picture up and held it close to his face. "Sure," he said, putting it back on the bar. "I've seen him in here a few times. Good tipper."

"Have you ever seen him here with another guy?"

"No, he always came in alone," he said. "Had a few drinks, maybe bought drinks for one of the ladies, but mostly kept to himself. A real quiet type."

"Yeah, he was a real gentleman," the blonde said. "Why are you looking for him?"

"It's a personal matter," I said. I pocketed the picture. "Thanks for the information."

I left her standing there with her mouth open as I walked away. It was probably the first time in her young life that a man hadn't fallen for her charms.

From Falls Church I took Lee Highway to the I-495 Beltway and drove west and north to the U.S. 1 exit, then, south on Highway 1 to Woodlawn, not too far from Fort Belvoir. *Jerry's Bar and Grill* was a rectangular building sitting in the middle of a large gravel lot just off the highway. It was well after

10:00 pm when I arrived, and the lot was filled with pickups, cars of all vintages, and a few vans, many with military base stickers in the windows. I parked near the building under a lamp post and made my way to the entrance. The heavy wooden door was flanked by plate glass windows that were painted over, blocking the view of the inside.

I pushed the door open and walked into a dark, cavernous space packed with people and the sound of music with a bass beat that caused my ears to buzz and my skull to vibrate. The smells of liquor, sweat, and tobacco were heavy in the air. When my eyes adjusted to the gloom, I could see that the crowd was mostly young, and mostly male, with enough buzz cuts to tell me that this was a GI hangout. A few older, grizzled looking types with the square jaws and broad shoulders of drill sergeants sat at tables along the walls. There were women there, about one for every five guys, mostly young, although a couple looked a bit long in the tooth, provocatively dressed, and cruising for drinks or dances.

No one paid me any attention as I made my way to the bar through the press of people. I found an empty slot and slid my body in, resting my elbows on the Formica top. The bartender, a middle aged man with close cropped hair that had more gray than any other color, came over and leaned across the bar until our heads were only inches apart.

"What can I get you, pal?" he yelled.

I took Lake's photo out and held it up for him to see. His eyes narrowed and he frowned. Just as he started to turn away, I pulled out my ID and showed it to him. Leaning across the bar, I shouted into his ear, "I'm working for his boss. He hasn't shown up for work in over a week, and the colonel he works for wants me to find him before the army treats him as an AWOL."

He looked intently at my ID, and then at me. Finally, he nodded. "Okay," he said into my ear. "But, we can't talk here. We can use my office in the back." He waved at an older woman with lank blonde hair who was standing at the end of the bar holding a tray in one hand and a towel in the other. She came over. "Roxanne, cover the bar for a while," he shouted at her. "I got some business to take care of."

She went around, ducked under the flip section of the bar. He bent and went under the section and motioned me to follow him.

14.

I followed him through a door in the back corner, into a well-lit hallway with two doors. He opened the one on the left and waved me in. When he closed the door the thud of music stopped, leaving us in silence.

The office, and calling it an office was being generous, was a tiny square space dominated by a gray metal desk in the center which was piled high with papers. A frayed and rusted gray upholstered metal chair sat to the side and a swivel chair with a broken arm was behind it. Boxes and piles of papers took up the rest of the floor space and spilled from the shelves lining the walls behind and to the sides.

The bartender took the chair behind the desk and pointed to the other chair.

"Have a seat, and tell me why you're looking for Rory Lake," he said. He had a no-nonsense tone in his voice.

There was no reason not to be somewhat

up front with him. I took out my ID and held it up. He snatched it from me and looked at it carefully before handing it back.

"So, Albert E. Pennyback, private investigator," he said. "I'm Jeremy Tuttle, Master Sergeant retired. Rory Lake is not only one of my best customers, but he's a damned fine NCO. Now, why is a private eye looking for him?"

"You know him well?"

"Yeah, we talk from time to time when he comes in, but, you didn't answer my question. Why are you looking for him?"

"I've been hired by his boss, Colonel Raymond, to find him," I said. "He hasn't checked in with his office since September Fourteenth."

"September Fourteenth?" He picked up a small calendar from the mess on his desk. "That was last Friday . . . he was in here that night, well, more like Saturday morning really. Came in late, had a few drinks and left."

"Was he alone?"

"No, he was with Morgan Freer." His mouth turned down when he said Freer's name.

"What can you tell me about Freer?"

"Other than the fact that I don't trust the sneaky son of a bitch and I think he was trying to snooker Rory into some kind of shady deal, not much."

He had my complete attention now.

"What kind of shady deal?"

"I didn't hear it all that clearly," he said. "I don't eavesdrop on my customers as a rule, you understand. Anyway, all I heard was Freer trying to get Rory to give him a copy of some report, and Rory saying he couldn't do it. Sounded like Freer wanted him to do something illegal."

"Did you . . . overhear this conversation the last time they were in here?"

"Yeah, that was it. They were standing down at the end of the bar, and every time I got near, Freer would stop talking. That's why I know it was something bad. There was one other thing . . . Rory's not a heavy drinker, but he really tied one on that last time he was here." I shot a querying look at him. "Around two in the morning, Freer had to help him out the door. He could hardly hold his head up. Funny, too, because I don't remember him drinking that much."

Morgan Freer was beginning to sound like someone I should be taking an interest in, enough interest to put Heather on his trail.

"Do you have any idea where the Morgan Freer character lives?"

"I'm not sure," he said. "I know he has a Fairfax County sticker on that black SUV he drives."

"You know what make and model?"

"Yeah, it's a '92 Ford Bronco, black or dark blue . . . no, I'm pretty sure it's black." His brow wrinkled. "You don't think that son of a bitch's done anything bad to Rory, do you?"

"At this point, Master Sergeant Tuttle, I don't know much, but I sure as hell plan to find out."

I left him sitting there with a look on his face that was a cross between worry and anger. I knew exactly how he felt.

15.

"Come on, Morgan," Rory Lake said, his voice muffled by the bag over his head. "Get this damn thing off my head. This isn't funny."

"It's not meant to be funny, Rory. It's meant to make you more cooperative."

Lake drew in a breath, almost gagging on the cloth as it was sucked into his mouth. The longer he sat there, his head encased, the less frightened and angrier he felt. "God damn it, Morgan," he said. "I'm not joking. Get this fucking bag off my head now."

He heard a shuffling sound, and then he felt hands on his shoulder.

"Listen up, soldier boy," Freer said gruffly. "You're not really in any position to be making demands or issuing orders. I'm not one of your fucking grunts. I'm in control here, and you better keep that in mind."

Lake breathed out slowly. *Got to stay calm. Morgan's lost his marbles. Don't want to tip him over the edge.* "Okay, Morgan," he said. "You're right, you're the man. But, could you please remove this bag. It's getting hard to breathe."

"I don't think that'd be such a good idea."

"Hell, why not? I already know it's you, so it can't be to keep me identifying you. And, if it's meant to make me do whatever you want, it's not gonna work. You want me to cooperate, take the fucking bag off my head, and maybe we can deal."

The silence stretched on for what seemed to Lake to be an eternity, before he felt the bag begin to slide up his head. When it was fully removed, even though the light in the basement was dim, after the darkness of the bag, it seemed like a floodlight. He blinked and then closed his eyes for a few seconds, then opening them slowly to allow them to adjust. When the stinging sensation stopped, he looked around. He was indeed in a basement, not unlike the unfinished basement of his own house. Bare concrete floor and naked beams and joists, and many dark corners. Off to the side, he saw a large furnace and water heater, the rusty pipes rising up and then running along beneath the floor boards. A single bulb hung from a ceiling beam, a low watt bulb from the lack of real light it put out.

Morgan Freer, mostly in shadow because the bulb was behind him, stood over him. Lake could make out the stubble on the square jaw, and could just see the man's fleshy lips and bent nose. He could imagine the cold blue eyes staring down at him.

"Okay, Lake," Freer said. "I took the bag off, now we can talk, right?"

"Sure, we can talk, but first, you mind telling me why you brought me here . . . how did you get me here without my knowing it . . . and, how long have I been here?"

Freer pulled a wooden chair over, turned it and sat straddle it, close enough that Lake could see the flakes of dandruff in his unkempt hair and smell the odor of stale liquor on his breath, which didn't help the stabbing headache he was suffering.

"You really don't remember anything?" Freer asked, blowing his stale breath in Lake's face.

"Uh, I seem to recall you came by my house and suggested we go out," Lake said. "We went to . . . Jerry's place. You were asking me about my work . . . I . . . I don't remember what happened after that."

"Damn, that shit really works."

"What shit?"

Freer chuckled and slapped his knee. "I gave you some ruffies. Got some pills from an old girlfriend of mine who had a prescription of Rohypnol for insomnia that I ground up and slipped in your whiskey when we were at Jerry's. I wasn't sure what dose a guy your size would take, so I gave you three. Worked like shit, man. You almost passed out before I got you out to the car, and you were out for three days."

"Morgan, man, why in hell would you do something like that?" Lake's anger was turning to confusion. "I thought you and me were friends."

"Aw, Rory," Freer said. "You're a good enough dude, but I gotta tell you, you're just a bit too straight-laced for my liking. I hooked up with you because I need information about that project you're working on over at Armcor."

"W-what do you know about Armcor?"

Freer patted his knee. "That's okay, buddy boy, you don't need to know that. You just need to tell me where you keep your notes about Loki is all."

Lake started feeling cold in his gut. He'd never questioned why Morgan Freer would start a casual conversation with him in Jerry's, or why he'd seem to pop up now and then and offer to buy drinks. A loner, Lake usually drank alone. Now and then, he'd buy a drink for one of the women who hang out at the bar, even go home with one now and then, but he'd never had male drinking buddies. Freer was funny, and he'd been good company. He'd never inquired about Lake's work until that evening . . . the evening he couldn't remember. He didn't have to remember, though, to know that he was in deep, deep shit.

16.

After talking to Tuttle, I decided to call it a night. I went home, took a shower to wash the smell of tobacco smoke and stale liquor off, and crawled in bed next to Sandra. She made moaning noises as I snuggled up to her. I didn't have the heart to wake her, so I just spooned and buried my face in her hair, and in a few minutes I drifted off to sleep.

We woke early – she woke up and roused me – and did our run and exercises, had a light breakfast, cleaned the kitchen together, and left in convoy, she to school and me to the office. We convoyed on River Road to the Beltway, where she kept on into the District, while I took the Cabin John exit to follow my usual route to work.

When I arrived at the office, I stopped at Heather's desk.

"How'd it go last night?" she asked.

I gave her a rundown of what I'd learned from Tuttle. "We need to locate this Freer character," I said by way of summing up. "Maybe the DMV records will have a current address."

"Sure they'll have it," she said. "The problem will be getting them to give it to us."

I smiled brightly. "That's why I'm asking you to do it. You'll find a way, you always do."

Of that I was confident. I went into my office to let her work without my interference. Before I could even sit down, though, the phone buzzed. I picked it up.

"Colonel Raymond for you," Heather said.

"Yeah, Bill, what can I do for you?"

"Al, I need to pay a visit to Armcor," Raymond said. "I'd like you to go along with me."

"What's up?" I asked.

"It's not something I can discuss over the phone. I'll tell you when we meet. I'll wait for you in the parking garage, or if you get there first, you wait for me."

He rang off without waiting for me to acknowledge his instructions. He sounded worried. He was paying the bill, though, so it was his call to make. I turned around and went out to my car.

He beat me to Armcor, but not by much, he was walking away from a blue Ford F-150 pickup as I pulled into the parking garage. There was an empty slot two down from his pickup, which he waved me into. I parked and walked back over to him.

"Okay, fill me in on the way to the lobby," I said.

He had a look of utter defeat and frustration on his face. "I took the puzzle magazine to General Bennington," he said. "He basically said it was bullshit, and that I needed something more substantial than scribbling in a magazine."

"So, you think coming here will get that something 'more substantial? You'll just let them know you know they're up to no good. That'll give them a chance to cover their tracks."

"Damn it," he said. "I know that, but I *have* to do something. I'm hoping maybe if we shake 'em up, they'll make a mistake or something."

I hate it when amateurs try to do my job. What he had in mind had about as much chance of working as a rabbit did of surviving living in a fox hole. But, he had a determined look on his face, so I knew I wasn't going to be able to talk him out of it. The best I could hope to do was minimize the damage.

"Okay, but you don't want to hit 'em head on. You need to go at them sideways . . . try to get 'em to say something incriminating. If you make a direct accusation, they'll just circle the wagons."

He stopped walking and stared at me. "I disagree," he said. "This is one where I think we should go right in their faces. See how they react. Hell, they have to know Lake knew, or at least suspected, something. What they don't know is how much, or how much he passed along."

"And, you plan to tell them?"

He laughed. "Of course not. What I do plan to do is dangle a few tidbits in front of them, and let 'em wonder how much more I know."

That brought me up short. As I ran it through my mind, it started to make a perverted kind of sense. He was right, of course. Armcor had to know that Lake was on to them, and they had to be wondering how much he knew and how much of it he'd passed along. Maybe shaking them up a bit was the way to go. It wouldn't be the first time I'd done something so unconventional.

"Okay, I'll go along with you," I said "But, if I see things starting to go haywire, you have to let me pull the plug."

"Deal," he said, and we shook hands.

I wondered how the minions monitoring us on their TV screens were interpreting what they were seeing, or if maybe they also had listening devices planted along the walkway as well.

We were about to find out.

Alec Sweeney was waiting for us in the lobby, florid faced and frowning.

"This is a bit irregular, Colonel," he said

as we entered. "We usually get more notice before a visit from the brass."

"A lot of things are irregular, Sweeney," Raymond said. "With Sergeant Lake unavailable at the moment, I decided an unannounced visit was in order. Take us up to Thissen's office."

"I'm not sure Ms. Thissen is available."

"That wasn't a request, Sweeney," Raymond said.

Sweeney reeled backwards a fraction of an inch. Raymond continued to glare at him. Finally, Sweeney shrugged.

"Okay, follow me."

He led us to the elevator and escorted us to the top floor. The same secretary was sitting at the same desk, doing nothing but looking good. She looked up when we stepped off the elevator. Her sculptured brows arched up.

"Alec, what are you doing here? I don't have any visitors on Mr. Winchester or Ms. Thissen's calendars," she said.

"We don't have appointments," Raymond said. "But, I feel sure both Winchester and Thissen will be available to me. I am, after all, the Pentagon supervisor of their main contract."

She gave him a pouty look. "Well, of course, sir," she said, her fingers poised over her space-age keyboard. "Who shall I say is calling?"

He made a growling sound deep in his

throat. I guess their intelligence system only worked for scheduled appointments. "Colonel William Raymond," he said. "Do you need to know which office I work in?"

The sarcasm was lost on her. "No, sir," she said. "Just the name is enough, thank you." She stabbed a button on the keyboard, and then typed rapidly on the letter keys. After a few seconds, she looked at the screen with a surprised expression. "Mr. Winchester will see you, colonel." There was a bit of astonishment in her voice and her expression changed to one of respect.

Raymond ignored her and strode to the door on her right. He pushed it open and walked in. I followed, with Sweeney close on my heels. Winchester was just standing. His office was, as I would have anticipated, even more opulent that Thissen's. Instead of diplomas and certificates, though, his walls were covered with photographs of him with various political notables – mostly of the ultra-conservative persuasion.

"Colonel Raymond," he said, coming around his desk with his hand extended. "Welcome." He pointed a finger at Sweeney. "Alec, could you get some chairs from Lila's office, and ask her to join us?" When Raymond had released his hand, he nodded at me and resumed his seat. Raymond sat in the chair on the left side of his desk. I took the one on the right. Thissen and Sweeney would have to take care of their own seating.

He only had two guest chairs. "Okay, colonel, what can I do for you?"

"There have been some questions about your last few field tests," Raymond said. "I need to review them to clear up a few points." The man wasted no time. He jumped right into the middle of it.

Winchester regarded him curiously, rubbing at his jaw. Not the reaction I would have expected.

"I don't understand, colonel," he said. "As far as I know, the tests were all just fine. What kind of questions?"

Raymond speared him with an icy gaze. "Sergeant Lake thinks the test results were manipulated."

Winchester rubbed harder at his jaw. "Manipulated? I'm afraid you'll have to explain that. How would we manipulate the tests?"

Leaning forward, Raymond smiled. If he'd smiled like that at me, I would have started looking for the nearest exit. Winchester leaned back in his chair and looked away.

"That," Raymond said. "Is why I'd like to get a look at the results myself. Lake thinks the successful fire rates and the circular error of probability rates were revised upward, but that in fact the actual results were unsatisfactory."

Before Winchester could answer, the door swung inward, and Thissen entered, followed close behind by Sweeney. Both carried straight back chairs.

"You wanted to see me, Haydn?" She looked down at Raymond, her shapely eyebrows lifting slightly. "Colonel, so nice to see you. To what do we owe the pleasure of a visit from the top brass?" She made an effort to keep her tone light, but I caught a nervous tension in her voice.

"The colonel seems to think the Loki test results have been somehow manipulated to make the craft look better than it is," Winchester said quickly. "I assured him that no such thing has happened."

"Why, of course not," Thissen said. "We conduct our tests with the utmost of integrity. What makes you think that, colonel?"

"Sergeant Lake believes your people have been cooking the results." Raymond turned in his chair and gazed icily up at Thissen. "That's why I'd like to see the original test results for myself."

"Sure, I have the reports in my office," she said.

"I don't think you understand what I mean," Raymond said, speaking slowly. "I don't want the damn reports your minions funnel up to you. I want the *originals*, and by that I mean the telemetry reports, ballistics charts, handwritten notes of the engineers—the whole damn shooting match."

Winchester and Thissen shared a brief glance. I was pretty damn sure I saw

Winchester shake his head, just the tiniest of movements, but a negative sign.

"Uh, I'm not sure we can do that," Thissen said. "I mean, the original data is after all proprietary."

"Lady, that fucking data belongs to Uncle Sam. We're paying for it, and it's ours."

She faced him, her head back, looking at him down the length of her nose. "Well now, I think we'll have to consult our legal counsel on that, Colonel."

Raymond's cheeks were red. He was either a good actor and getting into his role, or he was pissed. My money was on the latter. Thissen was being the stereotypical bureaucrat, not really saying no, but implying the hell out of it. Mostly, though, she seemed to be stalling for time, and I think Raymond knew it.

"Consult away, Lady," he said. "Just so you get me those damn papers within 24 hours. Come on, Al, let's get out of here so I can breathe some fresh air."

He stood abruptly and strode toward the door. I stood and hastened to follow, and Sweeney nearly fell off his chair trying to catch up with us. Good thing he did, too. Our theatrical exit would have fallen flat if we'd had to stand in front of an elevator that wouldn't come because we didn't have the proper security card to summon it.

Sweeney left us at the lobby exit. Raymond was quiet as we walked to the parking garage. As we arrived at his pickup, he turned and faced me, still frowning. Then, his face lit up in a broad grin, and he laughed. "How'd I do?" he asked. "Did I come off as the pissed off colonel?"

I looked at him. Damn if he wasn't enjoying himself. "You certainly convinced me," I said.

17.

Lake felt Freer's hot breath on the back of his neck. The man was so close he could feel the heat of his body and smell the rancid odor of sweat and stale breath.

"You had your chance, bucko," Freer said. "I was hoping the fucking ruffies would make you talk, but all they did was make you loopy. Now that they done wore off you getting all GI Joe on me, do I'm gonna have to get rough with you."

"Look, Morgan, I told you, the rules on disclosure are strictly need-to-know. Besides, it's pretty technical. You probably wouldn't understand."

"God dammit, you saying I'm too stupid or something?"

"No, man," Lake said hurriedly. "I'm just saying you have to understand a lot of technical stuff." Actually, he was saying Freer was too stupid. He couldn't believe he hadn't seen it earlier. It must have been the fact that he'd bothered to speak to him. Most of the guys in the bar ignored him. The only girls who paid any attention were the hookers or the ones Jerry paid to get the customers to buy them watered down drinks.

"I don't need to understand anyway. All you got to do is tell me where you put any notes you made."

Then, it hit him like a freight train running at full speed on a downgrade—Freer wasn't personally interested in Loki. Hell, he probably didn't even know or care what it was. He was working for someone, maybe Lila Thissen, and his job was to locate Lake's notes so they could destroy them. He wondered what Freer would do with him if he gave him what he wanted to know. *Damn, that was the wrong thing to think of. Only thing he can do is kill me. Shit, I'm up a creek in a leaky boat for sure. The only thing I can do is try and string him along as long as I can, until I can figure a way out of this.* "Look, man," he said. "I don't have any notes. I just saw some things that looked hinky, and I reported them to Colonel Raymond."

Freer laughed mirthlessly. "Now, now, bucko, don't try to shit a shitter. You're the type to write everything down, I know that. I been watching you. You're pretty organized. I know you got notes somewhere, and you gonna tell me where they are. You can do it the easy way, or the hard way. Don't make no fucking difference to me which way you chose."

"I. Don't. Have. Any. Notes."

"Okay, hard way it is."

Freer stood and walked out of Lake's range of vision. The young sergeant could hear scraping and bumping, and then Freer was back. In his hand was a large brown box with wires protruding from it. Alligator clamps were at the end of the wires.

Oh, shit! Not that! Anything but that! Lake clamped his legs tight. During anti-interrogation training, he'd been freaked by the stories of how the Communists were known to attach wires to a prisoner's genitals and then to a battery. He'd once been kicked in the nuts accidentally during hand-to-hand combat training, and it had hurt so he'd puked up his breakfast, and had walked bowlegged for a week. His body shivered at the thought.

But, instead of removing his pants, Freer ripped open his shirt, and then grabbed the neck of his T-shirt and yanked until the fabric split, exposing his nearly hairless chest.

'W-what the hell are you g-gonna do?" He could hear the fear in his own voice.

After exposing Lake's chest, Freer turned and pulled a strange looking device into view. It was a green box-shaped object on a tripod, with a hand crank on the side. It took Lake a few seconds to recognize the military model hand crank electrical generator. He hadn't seen one since his training days, but he remembered that the device could put out 220 volts of power, more than enough to kill a man, and certainly enough to hurt like hell.

Freer took his time connecting the wires to the generator. Then, he straddled the chair, holding an alligator clip in each hand and grinning wolfishly. "Okay, bucko," he said. "Last chance to be reasonable. Where are your notes on Loki?"

Lake gritted his teeth. He'd been taught to hold out, even under torture. Even though he'd never been subjected to electrical shock, since Freer wasn't going for his genitals, he reasoned he could withstand it for a while. "Sorry, Morgan," he said. "I don't have any notes."

"Now, that was the wrong answer, pal. I kinda figured you'd be all macho on me. You military types are all alike. Well, if you must know, I'm glad you did. I think I'm gonna enjoy this."

He reached over and attached an alligator clip to each of Lake's nipples. As the cold metal clamped down on him, Lake felt slight twinges of pain, but it wasn't unbearable, mostly just uncomfortable, like a bunion or corn in tight shoes.

As Freer turned and grasped the hand crank on the generator, Lake tried to relax and prepare himself. *I can handle this.* In that, though, he was wrong.

18.

I was back in my office the next day, sitting at my desk staring at the wall opposite without actually seeing anything and trying to get my mind around the case which was going nowhere.

Heather had blithely informed me that she was waiting for a response from her friend in the Virginia DMV in Fairfax, so she had nothing for me, which was her way of saying, 'get lost.'

I sat there willing the phone to ring—anything to give me something to do, when, the phone rang. I snatched it up. "Yeah, Heather, what you got?"

"Colonel Raymond to talk to you," she said curtly. I heard a clicking sound as she transferred the call.

"Al, are you busy?" Raymond said before I even had a chance to say hello.

"No," I said. "I'm just waiting for a break in this case. What do you need?"

"I just got a call from Thissen's office. She wants to meet us right away."

I couldn't see wasting any more time at Armcor. "Do you really need me there?"

"You were requested specifically. What do you say?"

I wanted to say that was strange. Why would the Armcor people want to talk to a low level bureaucrat? My curiosity antenna was raised. "Okay, I'm in. What time?"

"As soon as you can get there," he said, and rang off.

Thirty-five minutes later I'd passed the lift gate and parked next to Raymond's pickup in the back of the first level of the parking garage.

"What do you think they want with us?" I asked as I approached him.

"Your guess is as good as mine. The secretary called, and just said she wanted to see us right away."

"Well, let's get it over with," I said.

Sweeney was waiting for us at the end of the walkway instead of inside the lobby.

"Thanks for coming, gentlemen," he said. "Miss Thissen is waiting for us in her office."

"What's this all about, Sweeney?" Raymond asked.

"I have no idea." The security chief shrugged. "Miss Thissen just said you two were coming, and to bring you right up to her office."

He pushed the door open and ushered us through. We went straight to the elevators and preceded him for the trip to the sixth floor. One of the guys on the desk must have called ahead, because Thissen and a heavyset guy with what was left of his hair slicked back on a bullet head, and wearing an expensive gray silk suit waited for us at the elevator.

"Colonel Raymond, Mr. Pennyback," she said. "This is Vincent Peretti, Armcor's legal counsel." She inclined her head toward the guy in the expensive suit. "Would you please come with me to my office? Mr. Peretti has a few questions."

She turned and walked into her office. Peretti wheeled around and followed her. Raymond looked at me, his eyebrows raised. I shrugged and followed them.

Thissen was already behind her desk, glaring at us as we entered. Peretti stood in front of a chair to her right. Two other chairs sat directly in front of her desk. She pointed at them. We sat. For a moment, as she stood there looking at us, I felt like a misbehaving student called to the principal's office.

"I know you gentlemen are wondering why I asked you to come here," she said.

Out of the corner of my eye, I noticed that Raymond's expression had hardened. He was getting back into his previous day's role. "I hope," he said. "It was to tell us the reports I asked for are ready to be turned over."

"Hm, that will take a bit more time," Peretti said. "First, *I* have a question—why, Mr. Pennyback, did you pretend to be a DOD employee when you came here, and what did you do with the items you took from Sergeant Lake's office?"

19.

I pressed my lips together to keep from showing my shock. I'd been sure Thissen hadn't seen me slip the puzzle magazines into my shirt.

"What items? And, what do you mean, pretending to be a DOD employee?" I asked.

"You can stop the innocent act," Thissen said, sitting. "We know you're a private investigator." She speared Raymond with an icy look. "Really, colonel, sending a private eye in to check up on us? Why on earth would you do that?"

That caught Raymond off guard. He sat there with his mouth open.

"How'd you tumble to me?" I asked.

"It was simple enough to look you up," Peretti said. "You're written about frequently in the *Washington Post*. I believe they call you the Brown Knight."

That was true, but the question in my mind was, what made them even look me up.

There was no sense trying to deny it, though. "Okay, you got me." I turned to Raymond. "No sense trying to keep it up, Bill. You should tell them."

He looked determined—and not a little bit angry, but finally he sighed and turned to Thissen. "I sent Al in here because Sergeant Lake told me you guys were faking test results. I wanted to see if we could confirm what he told me."

Thissen smiled triumphantly. "And, of course, you found nothing."

"That remains to be seen," he said. "I still haven't seen those original documents."

"Ah yes," she said. "Speaking of documents, Mr. Pennyback, you stole documents from Sergeant Lake's office. We'd like them returned."

"I did no such thing."

She pointed a manicured finger at me. "Are you telling me you didn't take a magazine from Lake's office?"

I guess I hadn't been as slick as I thought. "Sure, I took a magazine from his book shelf," I said. "That's not quite the same as documents, though."

"It seems, though, that particular magazine contained notes that Sergeant Lake wrote that are proprietary in nature," Peretti said. "It therefore belongs to Armcor, and we're insisting that it be returned."

Now, that got my attention. I was willing to concede that Thissen might have

seen me take the book, but there was no way
she could have seen Lake's notes. She had to
have known about them in advance. That, of
course, left the question of why she hadn't
removed them earlier.

"So, Mr. Pennyback," she said. "Will
you return the magazine?"

"Sorry, but I don't have it anymore."

I looked her straight in the eye as I
spoke, so she'd know I was telling the truth.
She frowned, and looked at Raymond.

"It's not in my possession either," he
said.

Out of the corner of my eye I could see
that he, too, was looking straight at her. I
wondered how he could lie so glibly, until I
processed his words—he'd probably left the
magazine in his office, it's what I would have
done, so he was quite literally telling the
truth. She looked from him to me and back, a
puzzled frown on her face.

"What did you do with it?" she asked
us both.

"Al gave it to me, and I gave it to
General Bennington," Raymond said.

She smiled. "So, General Bennington
has it now?"

"Well, ah, no he doesn't," he said. Her
face fell. "I'm sorry that I can't tell you where
it is at the moment."

Again, he told the truth, except maybe
the part about being sorry.

She looked frustrated.

"Colonel," Peretti said. "This is a serious matter. You could get into trouble if you allowed proprietary information to get into the wrong hands. I must insist that you return this document forthwith."

"Well, Mr. Peretti, that's a bit of a problem. You see, I *can't* return these magazines to you forthwith, because one, I don't have them on me; two, I can't tell you where they are right now, and three, it's questionable whether a crossword puzzle magazine that Sergeant Lake purchased from the military post exchange with his own money can be considered a document belonging to Armcor."

"That, sir, is my legal opinion." Peretti puffed out his chest as he spoke.

"All well and good," Raymond said. "But, I'll have to get a legal opinion from the Pentagon legal counsels on that one."

"Look, Raymond," Thissen said. "Stop playing around. Return that document or there'll be trouble." Her face was red.

"That's *Colonel* Raymond to you, Ms. Thissen," he said evenly. "And, if you think I'm playing around, try pushing me to hard. Need I remind you that I'm in charge of your contract, and I can have all payments stopped immediately if I suspect something amiss?"

Her cheeks turned a darker red. "No, *Colonel*," she said. "General Bennington is ultimately in charge, and I think he'll have a different view of this matter."

She seemed awful sure of herself. That, along with her knowing what was in the magazine—or suspecting what was in it— made me want to know more about the general. To his credit, Raymond didn't flinch. He continued to regard her levelly, and when he spoke, his voice was steady.

"You can appeal to him if that's what you want to do," he said. "In the meantime, I think we've said all there is to say to each other." He stood. "Let's go, Al."

He turned, and with his shoulders squared, walked out. I smiled wolfishly at Thissen, and followed him. We waited patiently at the elevator for Sweeney, who had a perplexed look. The ride down to the lobby was done in silence, nor did we talk on the walk back to the parking garage.

When we arrived at his pickup, Raymond opened the driver's side door and motioned me close. As I stepped in, he reached across the seat and took the puzzle magazine from beneath the floor mat on the passenger side. He handed it to me, and I tucked it into my shirt. It'd been a long time since I'd done a surreptitious pass, but I still had the basics down.

"Put that somewhere no one can find it, and don't tell me where it is," he said quietly. "I have a feeling they're calling the general now, and he'll order me to return it. I'd like to be able to tell him I don't have it, and that I have no idea how to find it."

If not for the missing sergeant, this whole thing would have been a lark. I was enjoying giving the corporate hierarchy of Armcor the finger, and beginning to think General Bennington was one of those government bureaucrats in uniform who needed to be taken down a peg or two. If I could find Lake and make sure he was safe, I could really enjoy it.

20.

I got back to the office by 10:00. Heather smiled when I described the meeting at Armcor, and promised to redouble her efforts to find Freer, and hopefully Lake.

Before I could get to my office, the door opened and a beefy guy with a buzz cut and wearing a cheap suit walked in. I don't normally stereotype people, but this guy walked, dressed, and looked like a federal cop. Sure enough, as soon as he cleared the door, he took out a badge and held it up so both Heather and I could see it.

"Jack Sparr, Special Agent, Defense Investigative Service," he said. "I'm looking for an A.E. Pennyback."

"That would be me," I said. "What can I do for you?"

He looked past me at Heather. "Is there some place we can speak in private?"

Heather's blistering look was lost on him. Or, maybe he was just accustomed to it and ignored it.

"Let's go into my office," I said. I turned to Heather. "Hold all my calls, especially any from the colonel." I winked, and she smiled. I knew she'd be on the phone to Raymond as soon as I closed the door. I stepped aside and let Sparr precede me into my office, followed him in, and closed the door. I pointed to the chair near my desk. "Have a seat."

I took my time settling myself behind my desk. The guy was a pro, though, he showed no impatience, just waited stoically until I was comfortably leaning back in my chair.

"Tell me, Mr. Pennyback," he said. "What do the initials A and E stand for?"

That was a hell of a starting note, and frankly none of his damned business. Just for the record, they stand for Albert Einstein, thanks to my mother's obsession with the German scientist and her desire that maybe I'd go into academia. I'd learned to fight early because of that moniker. By the time I was in junior high school, I'd gained much of my full growth and was pretty good with my fists, so from that time, I'd been Al to anyone who didn't want a face full of fist.

"You can just call me Al," I said. "What can I do for you?"

He frowned at me. I guess he wasn't used to people not answering his questions, or turning them around and questioning him. He took a steno pad from his jacket and placed it on his knee.

"I understand that during a visit to Armcor, a company that has contracts with the Department of Defense, you removed material from one of their offices without their permission."

"If you're talking about the puzzle magazine," I said. "That's not exactly an official document, and since it was Sergeant Lake's personal property, I don't think Armcor has any right to it."

He scribbled something on his pad, and then looked up at me. "So, you admit taking it?"

"Yeah, I guess I do."

"So, you'll give it to me."

"No."

He opened his mouth. He closed his mouth. He looked at me with a kind of goggle-eyed expression. This wasn't going the way he'd anticipated.

"No?"

"You heard me. You have no more right to Lake's property than Armcor."

"And, you do?"

I'd pushed him off script, and he was floundering. I decided to push him a bit more. "Hey, it's just a magazine," I said. "When I see Sergeant Lake, I'll give it back to him."

He quickly wrote something on the pad. "Would you happen to know where Sergeant Lake is?"

"No, do you?"

"Uh? No, I don't," he said. "Officially, he's AWOL. When I find him, I'll have to take him into custody."

"Why do you say he's AWOL?"

"Because his commanding officer says he hasn't checked in like he's supposed to for over a week."

I knew that Raymond, who was his supervisor, not his commanding officer, since technically the commander of Washington Troops, the unit to which those individuals assigned to the Pentagon were assigned for housing, military justice and the like, was legally his commanding officer, hadn't reported him missing.

"Would you be referring to General Bennington?"

"Yeah, that's him," he said. "He's declared Lake AWOL. He has also decided that you have to return the magazine to Armcor."

"Well now, Agent Sparr," I said. "Maybe you have to follow the general's orders, but I'm a civilian, and I don't."

That was the final push. His expression went blank. I had him in a corner, and he knew it. He had to give it one final try, though. "Come on, I can tell from the way you carry yourself, that you spent some time in the army. You know how it is. Why can't you be reasonable?"

"If by be reasonable you mean roll over and do whatever I'm told, no thank you. You go back and tell your General Bennington I said . . . no, on second thought, don't tell him anything. I'm not giving you the magazine, and I'm not giving it to Armcor."

"Look, don't force me to involve local law enforcement."

I laughed. That was lame, and his expression said he knew I knew it. "Go ahead. I'd love to see you explain to some local cop that I stole a magazine from a missing man's office, and I'm a bad guy who won't give it back. I don't think the good general would appreciate that kind of embarrassment."

He was whipped. He knew it, and didn't like it. Slamming his note pad shut, he stood and shoved it back into his jacket. "This isn't over, Pennyback," he said. "You'll be seeing me again."

Heather had pushed open my door, and he brushed past her as he stormed out.

"What got into him?" she asked.

"He's upset because I won't come out to play with him," I said. "What's up?"

"I found Morgan Freer's address," she said.

Charles Ray

21.

The address Heather had gotten from her friend in DMV was southwest of the Beltway on Slidell Lane, not far from Lake Accotink. It was in one of the older neighborhoods, consisting mainly of ramblers and ranch styles built in the late sixties. Freer's house was a two level rambler set back from the street and surrounded by old growth oaks. The red slate roof was in bad need of repair, and the lawn hadn't had a good cutting in a while.

I pulled into the driveway, which was also in need of resurfacing, and turned the engine off. It was a working class neighborhood, so there weren't many people around. One or two pickups and vans in driveways I'd passed were the only signs of habitation. I got out and walked to the one car garage. I peered through the window. The garage was empty except for a rusty lawn mower and assorted tools hanging on nails in the wall studs.

I hadn't had a chance to take pictures during my visits to Armcor, but I thought it was time to start getting some graphic documentation, so I took the lighter-camera from my pocket and began taking pictures of the empty garage, the house, and the lawn.

I'd put the camera away and was heading back to my car, when an elderly woman dressed in denim overalls and carrying a garden trowel came around the side of the house.

"You looking for Morgan?" she asked.

"Yes, as a matter of fact, I am," I said. "He doesn't seem to be home."

"He hasn't been here for over a week." She looked around, frowning deeply. "You can tell from the condition of his lawn. He's too cheap to hire a lawn service, and he goes off for weeks at a time and lets it just go to pot. If you're a friend of his, you see him you tell him if he doesn't get this place cleaned up I'm calling the police on him."

"I'm not exactly a friend," I said. "I'm looking for him on a business matter. Do you know where he might be when he's not here?"

"Well, I hear his family had a farm off Highway 1 down south of Woodbridge. He used to go there on weekends and tend the place for his mother until she died last year."

I thanked her for the information, and after assuring her I'd deliver her message when I found Freer, I got back in my car and headed back to the office.

Charles Ray

22.

Heather looked up and frowned when I walked in. "I was just about to call you," she said. "Colonel Raymond wants you to call him immediately."

I didn't bother asking her why. If he'd told her she would have told me without my having to ask. I went into my office and dialed Raymond's number. He sounded worried when he answered.

"What's so urgent?" I asked.

"I've been given an ultimatum by General Bennington," he said. "If I don't get that magazine turned over to Armcor he'll bring me up on charges."

"He could never make them stick," I said.

"I know that, but just being charged will screw my chances of getting promoted. I hate to do it, Al, but I've got to ask you to give that damn magazine to Thissen."

"Dammit, Bill," I said. "It's the only evidence we have of their wrongdoing."

"Hey, pardner, I know that, but my hands are tied."

Then, I remembered the camera that I'd only used to take useless photos of Freer's house. It wouldn't be as good as the real thing, but a photograph could be pretty compelling evidence.

"Okay, I see the situation you're in. I'll meet you at Armcor at 1:00 this afternoon, how's that?"

He agreed and rang off. I took the magazine and camera out and got busy photographing every page, including the cover. When I was done, I gave the camera and cord to Heather to put on the computer. She suggested that we also print copies of each photo and put that file somewhere safe in the event of a computer malfunction. The woman earns her money and then some when it comes to computer stuff, which is mostly Greek to me.

"I need you to do one more thing for me," I said. "Morgan Freer might be at a place near Woodbridge that was owned by his late parents. I need you to get a location for me."

"That's all you have, somewhere near Woodbridge?"

I shrugged. "That's all Freer's neighbor could tell me. Can you do it?"

"Of course I can." She smiled. "It'll take a couple of hours. I'll have it for you by the time you get back."

Like I said, she earns her money, Heather does.

23.

I tucked the magazine in my jacket and left. On the way to Armcor, I stopped at a Burger King and got a Whopper with fries and an orange soda. After my grease fix, I drove to Armcor, arriving a few minutes after 1:00. Raymond was waiting for me at the entrance to the pathway.

"You brought the magazine?" he asked. There was a hint of urgency in his voice as if he worried I might renege on my agreement.

"Yeah," I said, taking it out of my jacket and handing it to him.

He looked relieved as he took it. "Okay, let's get this over with."

"Well, I see you gentlemen are back," Sweeney said as we entered the lobby. "Miss Thissen is waiting for you in her office."

He didn't offer to shake hands, so we both ignored him. He turned and we followed him to the elevator. We rode up to the top floor in silence. Thissen, an arrogant smile on her face, waited for us in front of the secretary's desk. Without a word, Raymond handed her the magazine.

She leafed idly through it, scanning the pages. I was pretty sure she quickly enough saw Lake's code. She probably already knew what he'd written. Finally, she walked over to a corner of the room where a large copier and a shredder stood, and slowly, she began ripping out pages and feeding them into the slot of the shredder, looking over her shoulder at us and smiling as she did it.

When she'd shredded the last page, she dusted off her hands and turned to us.

"Well, Colonel Raymond," she said. "So much for your evidence."

Still smiling, she turned and went into her office.

"I'd love to strangle that bitch," Raymond said under his breath.

"I wouldn't worry about it," I said quietly. "She'll get hers."

He looked at me with a quizzical expression. Then his face lit up in a half smile. "I should have known an old Green Beret wouldn't go down without a fight."

Sweeney looked at us with a confused expression. I didn't bother enlightening him.

24.

Heather had a big smile on her face when I walked into the office.

"You look like the cat that just got served canary on the half shell," I said.

"After you left to meet the colonel, I did a little snooping on his boss, and you'll like what I found out."

She was right about that.

In a short period of time, Heather had peeled back the onion that was Brigadier General Frank Bennington's life, exposing a bit of rot at the core that, frankly, surprised me.

Bennington, a graduate of West Point, had risen rather quickly to one-star rank, but then his career had stalled. Instead of being assigned to a combat unit like most of his classmates, he'd been consigned to a logistics desk in the Pentagon, his chance of a second star all but ended.

While interesting, that wasn't what caught my eye. It seemed that Bennington, married to his high school sweetheart and the father of three children, was living a secret life—or, at least a life that he thought was secret.

Heather had found a record of expenditures he'd made on weekend trips to New York and Philadelphia that were far beyond what even a brigadier general should be able to afford. A call to a friend of hers who worked for the city of Philadelphia revealed that his hotel stays in that city were accompanied by some very ritzy late night parties, and he was accompanied by a different young and beautiful woman on each trip. I had no doubt the same was true in New York. It appeared that the general was a randy old goat who was having several second flings in his later years, and I would have bet money that his wife and his bosses in DOD were unaware of it.

"What do you think of that?" Heather asked when she'd finished filling me in.

"I'm betting Armcor found out the same thing, and this explains their clout."

"You think they're blackmailing Bennington?"

"I do," I said. "Now, if only I could prove it."

"Let me do some more digging. My sources might know if there have been any other enquiries."

"Do you plan to tell Colonel Raymond? I mean, considering how much pressure Bennington's putting on him, it's only fair."

I thought about it. I figured I could trust Raymond not to misuse the information, and it might take the pressure off if he knew that we always had that card to play.

"Okay, you can call him and give him a censored version, just enough to make him feel better about things," I said.

"Good. Oh, one other thing. I have a location on the Freer place."

25.

It took me forty-five minutes driving down Highway 1 and then ten minutes on an unmarked dirt road to reach the gate across the road that marked the farm that had belonged to Morgan Freer's deceased parents.

I pulled the Volkswagen over to the side and got out. The fence was triple strand barbed wire set in metal posts. The gate was a wrought iron frame that was rusted from age like the fence posts, but the Yale lock securing it looked brand new. I checked carefully for booby traps, electrification, or any kind of surveillance devices, and found none. Freer obviously didn't want to be disturbed, but wasn't expecting any more than casual visitors, or maybe trades people. Being neither, I slipped through the strands of barbed wire and, kept to a thick stand of trees as I made my way in the direction I guessed the house to be.

The trees were thick near the fence, but thinned out as I walked. I came to the edge of the stand, finding myself about a hundred yards from an unpainted barn with several panels missing from its tin roof. Fifty yards beyond the barn was a small, two-story house set in the shade of a large, gnarled oak tree. A black Ford Bronco was parked in front of the wrap-around porch. I could see no movement, and the Bronco looked like it had been parked in the same spot for some time.

From where I stood, crouched beside a large tree, it was open all the way to the barn, except for a few bushes. Between the barn and the house there was no cover at all. There was no way I could approach the house during daylight without being seen.

My gut told me Lake was in the house, and that he was likely not there of his own free will. I'd learned during my years running covert recon teams in some pretty dangerous areas to trust those gut feelings—they'd saved my hide on more than one occasion.

I would have to wait until night to get inside the house. Another thing my gut was telling me was that this would be dicey as a one-man operation. I needed someone tough that I could trust to help me. Raymond was special operations trained, and he had a dog in the fight, but I just didn't know him well enough. That left only one other person to whom I could turn.

I moved back further in the trees and took out my mobile phone. I punched in a 202 number and held it to my ear.

"Detective Mayweather," a deep voice boomed in my ear. "How can I help you?"

"Buster," I said. "How'd you like to have supper with me at Mom's?"

Charles Ray

26.

After arranging the time to meet Buster, I called Sandra and let her know I'd be missing dinner, and would likely not be getting home until very late. She didn't ask me why. She'd been with me long enough to know that if I didn't go into detail during a phone call, there was a reason for it, and I'd always fill her in later. Besides, this way, she wouldn't be quite as worried as she'd be if she knew what I was up to.

I walked back to my car, made a U-turn and headed back to the District.

The traffic on Route 1 was heavy, but it was nothing compared to what I knew it would be on I-95. It nonetheless took me almost two hours to get to the Fourteenth Street Bridge, and then another thirty minutes from there to Mom's on Sixteenth Street.

It was nearly 6:00 when I arrived, and I had to drive two blocks to find a free parking space. By the time I'd walked back to Mom's,

Buster was already waiting for me at our usual table in the corner with a view of the street and the interior. He'd saved me a chair that backed on the wall.

Mom, wearing a yellow one-piece dress and a white apron, both of which stretched over her massive frame and contained enough fabric to make a tent that would sleep six, sat on a stool at the counter near the entrance where she could keep an eye on who came and went and the cash register at the same time. She smiled broadly when I entered.

"Hello there, boy," she said. "Ain't seen you in a long time. Where you been keepin' yourself?"

I gave her a hug and a kiss on her chubby brown cheeks, which caused her to giggle like a little girl. "Oh, I've been busy," I said.

"Well, it's good to see you. This the first time you come for supper, so I got a special treat for you. That old Buster done already got here, so you gone and set yourself down. You want coffee or ice tea?"

"I think iced tea would be better for supper."

She chuckled and pinched my cheek. I didn't even bother asking her what the special treat was, nor did I express a desire for anything else. When you're a regular at Mom's, you eat what she puts in front of you. Buster and I'd been frequenting her place for nearly a decade and I'd never been disappointed.

He waved as I approached the table. "It's 'bout time you got here, bro," he said. "I was just about to order without you."

"You've obviously only been here a few minutes," I said. "Or, you'd already have ordered."

"Hey, Mom," he said. "Can I get iced tea?"

"Sure can, hon," she fired back. "I figured you'd be drinking the same as your friend, 'cause he's got such good taste."

Mom was always ragging on Buster, and comparing him unfavorably to me, but in truth, she loved him like a son, and he knew it. She brought our tea. Mine was unsweetened, and I didn't have to tell her not to add sugar, while Buster's had so much sugar in it the brown liquid looked oily. Mom knew how we liked things.

He took a large swallow and sighed deeply. "Man, that really hits the spot." He put his glass down and propped his elbows on the table, resting his chin on his fists. "Okay, bro, you want to tell me what it is you want this time?"

Ordinarily I'd play with him a bit, but the matter was too serious for that. I told him my suspicion that the missing Sergeant Lake was being held at the farm near Woodbridge. "I was out there this afternoon," I said. "I can't get close to the house until after dark."

"Why didn't you just call the local police?"

"You're kidding right? Look, my first problem would be convincing them I'm not some wack job," I said. "And, then if I was able to convince them, that would be an even bigger problem."

"How so?"

"You've seen how all the police forces have been reacting since September 11," I said. "They see a terrorist behind every parking meter. If I convinced the cops that Sergeant Lake was being held hostage—and, I'm convinced that he is—they'd swarm in there with a heavily armed SWAT team and probably get him killed in the process. I hate to come down so hard on the cops, Buster, but you know how quick on the trigger some of these guys are. This operation, amigo, requires precision and stealth."

He opened his mouth to say something, but was interrupted by Mom's arrival with a tray heavily laden with our supper. Mom's a pretty savvy person, with people skills acquired after over thirty years slinging hash in the same location, so she knew we were having an important meeting. She quickly set our food and drinks in front of us, pinched Buster's cheek, winked at me, and made herself scarce.

For a few minutes, our attention was on the food. The special of the evening was breaded pork chops, home fried potatoes, red beans with little chunks of beef in them, and golden brown cornbread. The smell alone was enough to make my mouth water and my stomach jump for joy. We tasted bits of everything, making the appropriate noises of appreciation as the different tastes caressed our taste buds. It was probably bad for our arteries, but it tasted so good, I didn't care.

After that first rush of pleasure had subsided, we settled into our normal dinner routine, one talking while the other ate, and since I'd made a somewhat provocative statement that Buster felt obliged to respond to, I got the first crack at eating and listening.

"You telling me you plan to go in and try to rescue this dude by yourself?" he asked. The scowl on his dark face told me what he thought of that idea.

I put my fork down and finished chewing the food in my mouth. "Actually," I said. "I was hoping not to have to go in alone. This is the kind of operation where you need someone on your six."

He had a piece of pork chop halfway to his mouth. It stopped and hovered there while he looked at me sternly.

"You asking *me* to go with you? You know that's out of my jurisdiction."

"I think it's our best chance of pulling it off," I said. "A quick in and out, and with two of us, we ought to be able to do it."

"What if this Freer dude ain't working alone? What if I have to use my piece?"

He didn't ask about my using a weapon,

because he knew I didn't even own a gun, preferring to use my hands and feet. If I can't handle a threat that way, I use my feet to get the hell out of the way. I knew he wouldn't like what I was going to say next, though. "I wasn't planning on there being any gun play."

"Whoa, dude," he said. "You expecting us to go into an unknown situation with just our bare hands? Ain't that kinda dangerous?"

"We've done it before. Remember the time we took down that militia outfit in West Virginia? Look, Buster, we can do this." At the mention of our battle with a bunch of redneck militia men in West Virginia several years earlier, some of his skepticism evaporated. "Besides, like you said, it's out of your jurisdiction. Imagine the stink if you should shoot someone."

"Okay, but if I do this and you get me hurt, Alma's gonna kill you, right after she kills me."

Buster's wife, Alma, was a tiny woman, about half his size, but she was a spitfire, and she scared the hell out of him. "I promise to keep you safe," I said. "I basically need you to create a diversion anyway. Just enough to allow me to get inside the house and find Lake."

"Fine," he said, sighing. "When we gonna do this?"

"I have a gut feeling about it that tells me there's no time to waste. I'm thinking midnight tonight."

"Well, at least I don't have to rush my meal."

27.

Lake hurt all over. His body had bucked so hard every time Freer turned the generator hand crank he feared he'd torn some muscles. He'd held out as long as he could, but the pain was just too much, and he'd finally told the man what he wanted to know. Finally, the torture stopped, but the pain went on and on. Worse, he had a blinding headache, so bad he felt like he would vomit if he didn't get some ease.

After removing the alligator clips from his chest, Freer had moved the torture device out of Lake's line of sight and left the basement. Left alone, with nothing but the single light bulb suspended from a ceiling beam for light, Lake lay still for a long time.

As he became accustomed to the dull pain, he began to think clearly. Now that Freer had what he wanted from him, Lake knew his usefulness was at an end. The man could hardly let him walk free.

He squirmed around on the chair to find

a more comfortable position. As he did so, he noticed that the ropes around his arms were not as tight as before. He strained against them. It seemed like he'd been tied up in this dim, dusty place for days, but for the first time since waking up he felt a glimmer of hope.

His wrists were burning and the muscles in his shoulders ached. He'd been working at the ropes for what felt like hours, and they didn't seem any looser.

He heard the creaking of the door at the top of the stairs opening. A gray rectangle of light illuminated the stairs which he could just see out of the corner of his vision if he strained his head around to the left. For a moment, before the door was closed and the light disappeared, he saw an elongated shadow. Freer was coming back. He felt a chill in his gut. *Damn rope's still too tight.*

As Morgan Freer moved into his view, he stopped straining at the ropes around his arms. He looked up at the hulking figure. In the dim light he could just make out his facial features. What he saw gave him a chill all over.

Freer looked down at him, a vulpine smile on his face. "Well, bucko, I guess we're done here," he said. "Looks like the information you gave me was good."

Lake's throat was dry, and when he spoke, his voice was strained and cracked. "So, you're gonna let me go now?"

Freer laughed—a harsh sound without mirth—and it made Lake shiver. He'd heard it said that in situations when death was imminent, a person's life flashed before his eyes. That was a lie. All he could think of was getting the hell out of that chair.

"Sorry, Rory old buddy," Freer said. "Much as I'd like to let you go, I really can't afford to."

"H-hey, man, you don't have to do this. I won't talk to anyone, I swear."

"I'd like to believe you, man, I really would. I sort of took a liking to you. But, a job's a job, and I have to tie up all the loose ends. You, my friend, are one of those loose ends."

Lake opened his mouth to protest, when in his peripheral vision he saw a large figure step off the bottom step and move silently in Freer's direction. He closed his mouth when the figure, a dark man with close cropped hair and broad shoulders, dressed entirely in black, put a finger to his lips.

Freer leaned forward, pulling a switchblade from his pocket. "I'll try to make this as quick and painless as possible, buddy," he said.

"I think not," a deep voice said from behind Freer.

Charles Ray

28.

After we finished eating, Buster took off and I drove home. Sandra watched wide-eyed as I pulled on my night-work gear, black cargo pants, black sweat shirt, and my black commando boots. I put a set of lock pick tools in one of the leg pockets on my pants, and my sheathed K-bar knife in another. When I was done, I walked over to where she stood by the bed and pulled her into my arms. I just held her close, feeling the heat from her trembling body as she clung to me. After a long time just standing there, I tilted her head back and kissed her lightly on the lips.

She reached up and touched my cheek, letting her finger slide slowly down to the jawline. Her eyes glistened in the light from the lamp by the bed.

"Be careful, my darling," was all she said. I kissed her again.

I rendezvoused with Buster near the U.S.

Highway 1 ramp off I-495. He was driving a bright red 1982 Chevrolet Trans-Am, not exactly an appropriate car for a man with two children, but when it comes to cars, Buster prefers flash and style to what's appropriate. Fortunately, he'd bought a Buick Estate station wagon for Alma and the kids. I pulled in behind him and flashed my lights.

I got out, and as I approached his car, he rolled the window down. He was wearing a pec-hugging black pullover and a black skull cap—looking ready for action.

"You all ready for this?" I asked.

He grinned up at me. "Let's rock and roll."

"Okay," I said. "Follow me."

He rolled his window up and started the Trans-Am. The souped-up engine growled.

My Volkswagen couldn't match the Trans-Am for macho sound, but I'd had the engine reconditioned, so it wasn't exactly a pussy cat. As I pulled past him, I put it in neutral and pushed down on the gas pedal to give him a taste of what the Bug could do. As I put it back in gear and accelerated down Route 1, I could see the Trans-Am behind me leaving a trail of smoke as its heavy duty tires bit into the asphalt. I couldn't see his face in the dark, but I knew Buster was grinning broadly. He was enjoying this.

The traffic between Alexandria and Fort Belvoir was pretty heavy, but once we passed the big army base, it thinned out, consisting mainly of pickups and a few trucks whose drivers had decided to give I-95 a pass. We made good time to the turnoff just north of Woodbridge. It was just before midnight when we arrived at the gate. I pulled over, doused the lights and turned off the engine. The throaty growl of Buster's car echoed in the night air for a few seconds, and his heavy duty headlights lit up the dirt road beyond the gate before being turned off and momentarily plunging me into darkness. I hoped no one in the house beyond the trees was near a window, or, heaven forbid, outside the house. There was no way they wouldn't have heard that, or seen the flash of light through the trees.

For a big man, Buster can move almost as quietly as I can. By the time I got out of the car and was stretching my muscles, he was beside me. The moonlight provided just enough illumination for me to see that he was smiling in anticipation.

"It's a few hundred yards through the trees to the house," I said quietly. "The last stretch, though, is over open ground. We need to move fast, but quietly at the same time."

"Lead on," he said.

Charles Ray

29.

We made good time through the stand of trees. I halted at the edge and knelt. Buster knelt beside me.

Details were hard to make out even with the moonlight, but I could make out the Bronco still parked in front of the house. There were no lights visible in the upper floors, but I could see a slight orange glow along the foundation—just a small rectangle of light at ground level to the right of the front porch.

"Looks like a basement window," Buster said. "Probably got a door down to the basement near the front of the house."

That made sense. While there was a high probability that Freer and Lake were the only ones in the house, and both were in the basement, I couldn't rule out the possibility of someone else being present. There was a lot of open ground to cover, and someone looking in the wrong direction as we were crossing it could blow the whole operation.

"Okay," I said. "I'll take the front. You work around back and see if you can find a way in . . . quietly."

"I might not have been trained by the army like you," he said. "But, I know how to move without sounding like a herd of cows." He chuckled and slapped me on the shoulder. Then, like a dark shadow, he moved to the right and disappeared behind a large clump of bushes. Except for a slight whispering sound as his body brushed the foliage, he was silent.

It was time for me to make my own move. I took a deep breath, and then sprinted for the edge of the barn. It sat at a slight angle to the house, so I was able to move to the far corner of the front from where I could peek around and see the house. There was still no indication of any presence on the ground floor, and I couldn't see any flickering indicating movement in the basement.

The last stretch, from the barn to the edge of the front porch, was about a ten to fifteen second run, but the nagging feeling of being watched from the house made it seem longer. I moved to the left, keeping the porch between me and the basement window, and knelt while I caught my breath.

The only sounds were the creaking of wooden boards in the cool night air as they lost heat and contracted, and the chirping of night creatures in the nearby woods. So far, so good.

I eased to a standing position and tested the wooden steps of the porch. They were solid, and only creaked slightly as I slowly stepped up. The floor of the porch was made of tightly fitted wooden planks that also creaked a bit as I took the three steps to the front door. Once there, I stood silently with my ear close to the wall. I heard no sounds of movement from inside the house.

The screen door hinges squeaked when I slowly pulled it open, forcing me to wait again to make sure I hadn't alerted anyone in the house to my presence. After a moment of silence, I knelt and, taking the lock picks from my pants, began working on the door lock. It was an old single cylinder deadbolt which took me about forty seconds to open. The wooden door swung open silently, and I walked into a small foyer that fronted onto a living room. I pushed the door shut and stood there for a while to let my eyes adjust to the low light level.

After a while, I could make out the details of the room with the small amount of moonlight that filtered through the curtains. To the left was an archway that led into a dining room and to the right a staircase leading to the second floor. There was a door in the wall beneath the staircase, which I guessed would lead to the basement.

The floor in the foyer and living room was

bare wood, so I kept to the wall as I made my way to the staircase to keep from making noise on the floor, which would be easily heard by anyone in the basement.

At the staircase, I put my ear against the door. I could hear muffled voices, but couldn't make out what was being said.

There was a slight scratching sound and a shadow appeared to my left. I recognized Buster's outline as he moved past the lower steps of the staircase to stand next to me.

"I jimmied the kitchen door and got in," he whispered. "Nobody's back there."

"There's someone in the basement," I said. "I'm thinking I should check that, while you make sure no one's upstairs. I'd hate to be surprised."

"You sure you want to go down there alone?"

I put a hand on his arm. "I think I can handle it."

I was tempted to tell him to be quiet going up the stairs, but I knew that would only piss him off. He moved quietly enough for such a big man, and he knew the drill. He moved to the bottom of the stairs and started up, keeping his feet on the ends of the steps to keep from making sound. He moved slowly, but still made good time and was quickly out of my line of sight. I turned my attention back to the door.

Slowly, very slowly, I pulled the door open. When I had it open just wide enough, I slipped through. Sure enough I was at the top of wooden steps leading down into a basement. I eased the door shut, and started slowly down.

The voices were now clear.

Charles Ray

30.

Halfway down the steps by the light from a single bulb suspended from the ceiling beams I saw the source of the voices. A light brown skinned man sat tied to a chair. A large white man stood over him. From where I stood I could see the fear in the man in the chair. The man in the chair was Rory Lake, which meant the standing man had to be Morgan Freer.

"I'd like to believe you, man," the white man said. "I really would. I sort of took a liking to you. But, a job's a job, and I have to tie up all loose ends. You, my friend, are one of those loose ends."

Lake opened his mouth. Then, his head turned and he was looking directly at me. I put a finger to my lips and shook my head. His eyes went wide, but I could see some of the fear leave his expression.

The white man pulled a switchblade from his pants pocket. There was a 'snick' as he pressed the button on the handle, and a nine-inch double edged blade shot out.

"I'll try to make this as quick and painless as possible, buddy," he said as he moved the knife toward Lake's throat.

I stepped off the stairs and moved toward him. "I think not," I said.

The man, my height with probably twenty pounds on me, whirled around, the knife held at his waist in his right hand. He glared angrily at me. "Who the fuck are you? How'd you-"

"Doesn't matter who I am," I said, cutting him off. "Now, why don't you just drop the knife before someone gets hurt?"

He went into a classic knife fighting stance; bent slightly at the waist, his feet shoulder width apart, the left foot slightly forward, left hand out to his side with the palm in toward his body, and the right hand—holding the knife with the blade tilted slightly upwards—in front of his body. He'd done this before. But, then, so had I.

"The only one's gonna get hurt, fuck wad, is you," he said as he shuffled toward his right and slightly toward me.

He might be experienced in knife fighting, but he didn't know beans about combat. In combat, you save your breath. You don't tell your adversary what you're going to do to him, you save your energy and do it. This guy got his experience on the street. I received mine on the battlefield.

I waited, shifting only enough to keep him directly in front of me.

My actions, or my lack of action, must have unsettled him. He got a worried look in his eyes. Maybe he expected me to either run away, or charge him—or at least, look scared—instead, I locked gazes with him. He didn't know it, but I had the advantage. He had probably never faced anyone who wasn't afraid of him, while I'd faced a number of people who wanted to kill me.

I continued to wait for his move. His eyes flickered, and his gaze dropped for a millisecond toward his right hand. His left hand moved farther away from his body and his palm turned toward the floor. When his right heel lifted from the floor and he started forward, his right hand thrusting toward my gut, I made my move.

It wasn't the move he'd expected, which was ducking back from his knife thrust. Instead, I swung my left foot back and pivoted my body to the left, allowing the knife to slice through air where my body had been. It almost touched the fabric of my shirt. As he reached the full length of his thrust, I grabbed his wrist with my left hand from underneath, and got a grip on his upper forearm with my right hand from above. At the same time, I pushed down with my right hand, and brought my right leg up, knee bent, slamming his arm across my thigh with all the force I could muster. I was rewarded with a loud cracking sound, followed immediately by a piercing scream as the pain at the point of fracture in his forearm traveled along the nerve paths to his brain. His fingers went limp and the switchblade dropped to the floor. I maintained my grip on his wrist, but removed my right hand from his arm and chopped at his Adam's apple with the side of my hand, cutting him off in mid-scream. His left hand went to his throat and his eyes bugged as he coughed and tried to breathe.

I brought my left knee up and punched it against his gut. That got him breathing, but also brought on another scream, which I stopped by slamming my right fist into his jaw. He went down, his head bouncing off the floor and kicking up a little cloud of dust. He lay still.

Buster came bounding down the stairs with his service revolver in his hand.

"What the hell?" He stopped, and looked down at Freer's prostrate form. "Oh, I see you got him."

"Yeah, and I thought I said no guns."

He looked at the pistol in his hand, and back at me with a guilty smile. "Sorry, bro," he said. "I just feel naked without it. Never go anywhere without these either." And, he pulled a pair of handcuffs from his pocket.

I couldn't restrain a laugh. "I guess they will come in handy. Go ahead and truss him up before he wakes up."

"He ain't gonna be waking up for a while."

"Uh, guys," Lake said. "Could one of you untie me, please?"

Darn! I'd almost forgotten the reason we were in the basement in the first place. I hurried over and, taking out my K-bar, began cutting Lake's bindings. "You okay?" I asked him as he rubbed his wrists to get circulation back in them.

"I am now," he said. "I don't know who the hell you guys are, but I'm sure glad you showed up." He looked confused. "By the way, what are you doing here?"

I told him what his boss had hired me to do. When I'd finished, he looked worried.

"You gave Lila Thissen my magazine?" he said. "Now, I don't have any proof that they've been faking the test results. That was the only record I made."

"Not to worry, sergeant," I said. "I took photos of every page. I have to check with my lawyer friend, but I think those photos with you to certify their authenticity will be enough to fry Ms. Thissen and Armcor good."

"What are we gonna do with our friend here?" Buster asked.

"Put him in the chair here," I said. I helped Lake to stand. "Before we turn him over to the local law, I'd like to ask him a few questions."

I helped Buster manhandle Freer into the chair, and after splashing his face with water and waking him up, asked him a few pointed questions. He was groggy at first, and refused to cooperate, but after a few taps on his broken forearm reminded him who he was dealing with, he sang like a tenor trying out for the opera. What he had to say was interesting. It was guaranteed to spoil a few peoples' day.

When I was satisfied that he'd told us all he knew, I let Buster call the cops. He'd drugged and kidnapped Lake in one county, and held him hostage in another, so Buster called the Virginia State Police, who, when they learned of the military connection, called in the FBI. Another bit of fallout from 9-11. Local cops were more willing to work with the feds, because the government was funneling money to those who were cooperative. It took us a bit of tap dancing to explain how we came to be on the scene to rescue the kidnapped sergeant. The fact that Buster knew the senior state cop on the scene helped. After the paramedic checked Lake out and gave him electrolytes for his dehydration and salve for the electrical burns on his chest, the feds took his statement, further burnishing Buster and my credentials as good citizens who came to his rescue.

After Freer had been carted away by the FBI, for further interrogation, I thanked Buster for helping me out, put Lake in my car and drove him home. After we arrived, I called Raymond and made arrangements for him to meet me and Lake at my office the next morning. I told him to prepare for a long and interesting day.

I offered to take Lake to my house and let him sleep on my couch, but he assured me that he'd be okay. He was a tough one, and was already recovering from an ordeal that would have broken a lesser person. I gave him directions to my office and told him to meet me there at 9:00. It was already 3:00 am, which didn't give either of us much time to sleep, but we had things to do that couldn't wait. Sleep could come later.

Charles Ray

31.

I got to my office at 8:45 the next morning. I'd passed on my usual morning run, and had just toast and coffee for breakfast, so I was a bit groggy and out of sorts. Heather recognized that, so when I walked in, she shooed me into my office and followed immediately with a cup of tea, which she insisted I drink. It was a bit too flowery, but soothing, so I drank it without my usual grumbling.

Lake arrived at 9:00 sharp. He looked none the worse for experience. In fact, in his khaki service uniform, he looked pretty spiffy. He certainly got Heather's attention. She nearly tripped over herself getting him a cup of tea.

She hovered over him as he sipped. "Is there anything else I can get for you?" she asked.

I'd never seen Heather act this way before. I ushered Lake into my office. "Have a seat, sergeant," I said. "I have something I need to talk to my partner about, and I'll be right with you."

I closed the door and turned to Heather. "You okay, Honeybunch?"

She was staring at the closed door. "Uh, huh?" She shook her head. "Sure, I'm okay," she said. "So, that's Sergeant Lake? He's kinda cute."

"Ah ha, you're kinda smitten by him, aren't you?"

She scowled at me, but her cheeks were red. "Am not. W-what makes you say that?"

"Oh, come on, don't play coy with me. I see the way you're looking at him. Nothing wrong with that. He is a good looking kid."

"He is that," she said. "B-but, he's probably already spoken for."

"Not that I know of." Her smile lit up like the stage lights at Kennedy Center. "But, right now, we've got work to do," I said. "You can play later. I need you to call Quincy and tell him I'm coming over with Lake and Raymond as soon as Raymond gets here, and I need the copies you made of the magazine page photos."

"Okay." She pouted. "I'll bring the photos in as soon as I call Quincy. You want me to send the colonel in when he comes?"

I nodded and went into my office. Lake was sitting in the chair near my desk, staring at the door with a goofy smile on his brown face.

"Your partner," he said. "Is she married, or seeing anybody?"

I rolled my eyes, and laughed. The two of them were acting like junior high school students at their first dance. "No, sergeant, she's neither. And, if you must know, she's kind of interested in you too."

He looked at me, first with an expression of disbelief, then a broad smile. I'd just made his day.

I put up with them making eyes at each other when Heather brought the photos in. When she'd gone, I asked Lake if he recognized the photos. He agreed that he did and complimented me on my photo taking skills. We'd just gotten through the last photo when Raymond walked in, followed by Heather.

"Quincy's waiting for you," she said. She was talking to me, but she never took her eyes off Lake.

"Okay, guys, let's go," I said.

Lake almost tripped over his own feet going out the door. He never took his eyes off Heather.

I overruled the both of them, and we used my Volkswagen rather than one of their pickups. I couldn't see trying to park either of them in the basement garage of the building Quincy's law firm was in. As the smaller of the three, and the most junior, Lake got the back seat, while Raymond, who had legs as long as mine, squeezed into the front passenger seat.

It took twenty minutes to get from my office to Quincy's K Street skyscraper, and we managed to find parking adjacent to the elevator. We rode to the top floor where Holcombe, Stein, and Chang had its offices. A young man at the front reception desk, after satisfying himself that I was who I said I was and that I was authorized to escort two people into the law firm's inner sanctum, let us pass through to the hallway in which the three partners had their offices. Quincy's purple-haired, indeterminate age personal assistant, upon seeing Rory Lake, simpered and puffed out her not inconsiderable chest at him rather than flirting with me as she usually did. If I was an insecure person, I'd start to dislike the young sergeant.

Quincy, his jacket off and his vest unbuttoned, waited for us behind his desk. He stood and shook hands with Raymond and Lake, and waved at me.

"Gentlemen, have a seat," he said. "Would you like coffee?"

Raymond and Lake both accepted coffee, which Quincy had his assistant bring in. I passed. So did Quincy.

"We need your legal advice," I said to Quincy when everyone had their cups and were seated. "We have photographs of a document that Sergeant Lake here created. I need to know if it would hold up in court."

"Do you have the documents with you?" Quincy asked.

I passed him the photos. His eyebrows arched upwards. "Are these-?"

"Yes," I said. "These are photos of the pages of a puzzle magazine. But, look at them more closely."

As he did, comprehension dawned, and he smiled. "Ah, I see. So, Sergeant Lake, I assume you wrote this? Can you swear these are photos of the pages you wrote?"

"Yes, sir," Lake said. "That's my writing."

Quincy handed the photos to me. "In that case, they'd carry just as much weight at the originals would. The key is your credibility, sergeant. If you're convincing, then they would be accepted."

That's what I needed to hear. "Thanks, Quincy, I owe you a big one for this," I said. "Okay, guys, let's go pay a call on our friends at Armcor."

Quincy stood and fixed me with a stern gaze. "I don't suppose you're going to tell me what this is about, are you?"

"Later, amigo," I said. "Right now, we've got some fish waiting to be hooked."

He winced. "On second thought, I'm not sure I really want to know."

Thirty minutes later, we pulled in front of the drop gate leading to the Armcor parking garage. Unlike our past visits, this time the gate stayed down.

"So," Raymond said. "What do we do now?"

I turned the engine off and got out of the car. "We leave the damn car here, and we go inside," I said.

The gate began to rise. So, they did have listening devices planted in the garage. I got back in and drove in. I found an empty slot near the entrance to the walkway. We got out and walked to the front entrance of the building. Sweeney was waiting for us just inside the door.

He had dark circles under his eyes, and his suit looked like he'd slept in it.

"Okay, what the hell do you guys want?" When he recognized Rory Lake, he went a bit goggle-eyed. "Sergeant Lake, where have you been?"

"For your sake, Sweeney," I said. "I hope you really didn't know."

"W-what is that supposed to mean?"

"It means we want to see Lila Thissen. Right now. Colonel Raymond, would you also call Special Agent Sparr at DIS? I think he might want to be here. I should have thought to invite him earlier."

Raymond pulled out his phone and stepped off to the side to call. After a hushed conversation, he returned his phone to his pocket and came back to stand beside me. "He'll be here in twenty minutes," he said.

"Do we wait for him?"

"Let's wait," I said. "You mind, Sweeney?"

The security chief was standing there staring at Lake, his mouth gaped open. "Uh, huh? No, it's okay if you want to. Should I call Miss Thissen and let her know you're here?"

"No, let's wait for Sparr. He really should hear everything I think."

"Suit yourself," he said. "We're not exactly set up here in the lobby for lounging."

By the time Special Agent Jack Sparr strode through the lobby door, I was tired of standing around looking at the bored security guards who were probably just as tired of looking at me. He walked over to Raymond, a frown on his craggy face. "Okay, colonel, I'm here," he said. "What's going on?"

"Come with us upstairs," I said. "All will become clear then."

He gave me a skeptical look.

"Trust him, Agent Sparr," Raymond said. "You won't be disappointed."

His expression said he didn't believe that, but Raymond was senior officer present, so he just shrugged.

"Okay, Sweeney, you can take us up now," I said.

When we arrived at the top floor, I had Sergeant Lake stay behind us as we walked out of the elevator. The secretary looked up, a surprised expression on her face.

"Alec, what's up? Neither Ms. Thissen nor

Mr. Winchester have meetings on their schedules."

"They're here on special business, Felicity," Sweeney said. He turned to me. "I guess you want to see Miss Thissen first?"

"Yeah, we do," I said.

"B-but, you can't just barge in," the secretary said.

Jack Sparr pulled his badge and held it up in front of her face. "Yes, we can, Miss," he said. "And, if you know what's good for you, you won't touch any of those buttons on your desk."

Her mouth popped open and rapidly shut as she took in his gold badge. She sat down and put her hands in her lap. I walked to Thissen's door and pushed it open.

Lila Thissen, wearing a lime green pant suit, was sitting behind her desk, thumbing through papers in a brown folder. As we walked in, she looked up, frowning.

"What's the meaning of this," she said. "You don't have an appointment, and I'm very busy."

"I suggest you clear your calendar, lady," I said. "Colonel Raymond and Agent Sparr here have important business to discuss with you."

"I don't care what you suggest, Mr. Pennyback. I only see people by appointment."

"No, Ms. Thissen," Raymond said. "I want to discuss your falsifying test data on Loki, so you *will* speak to us."

She laughed harshly. "Really, colonel, are you going to persist in beating that dead horse. You have absolutely no evidence of your allegations, so why don't you gentlemen get out of here and let me get back to work."

I waved Raymond and Sparr aside, exposing Rory Lake to her. Her eyes went wide and the color drained from her face.

"Actually, Ms. Thissen," I said. "We have all the evidence we need. Isn't that right, Sergeant Lake?"

I took the photos out of my jacket and held them up.

"Right as rain, Mr. Pennyback," he said. "You got the photos of my notes right there."

"Can I see those?" Sparr asked.

I handed them over. After reading the first three or four, he looked at Thissen, frowning deeply.

"You care to explain this, Ms. Thissen?"

She looked like she wished she was anywhere but on the spot where she stood. I don't think she even heard his question. Her eyes had never left Lake.

"Oh, I think Ms. Thissen has more to explain than a few faked test results," I said.

"What do you mean by that?" Sparr asked.

I walked around the desk and stood next to Thissen. She looked at me. Her expression was crestfallen. A single tear formed in the corner of her left eye. It was almost—just almost—enough to make me feel sorry for her. But, not enough, not by a long shot. She had sins to answer for.

"You want to tell him, or shall I?" I said.

She began to tremble. She reached blindly behind her for the arms of her chair, and slowly she sat, looking beaten and deflated.

"Okay, I'll take that to mean you don't want to talk, so I'll do it," I said. "Ms. Thissen, in addition to defrauding the government, is also guilty of conspiracy to commit kidnapping and murder. Thankfully, my friend Buster Mayweather and I were able to intervene before the murder. Oh, and I guess she's guilty of conspiracy in assault and battery, or torture, too. Which would you call it Sergeant Lake?"

Lake's face was cold. "Oh, definitely torture," he said. "That son of a bitch attached electrodes to me and ran electrical current through my body."

Sparr was now looking totally confused. He looked from Lake to me and back again like a spectator at a tennis match.

"Sergeant Lake was abducted by a man named Morgan Freer," I said. "Freer tortured him to extract information about the sergeant's notes on what Armcor was doing with the Loki tests. Fortunately, we found him just as Freer was about to kill him—on orders from Ms. Thissen here."

"T-that's not true," she said weakly.

"Did Freer tell you Thissen gave him the order to kill the sergeant?" Sparr said.

"That, and more," I said. "I had a nice chat with him before the feds arrived and took him into custody. I imagine he's told them even more."

"I guess that takes General Bennington off the hook," Raymond said. "When she asked for the magazine, and then shredded it, I was sure he'd been the one to tell her about it."

"So was I," I said. "But, you're wrong about it taking him off the hook. He still had to know, or at least suspect, that Sergeant Lake's information was valid, and he tried to cover it up."

"And, it was the general who declared the sergeant AWOL and had us called in," Sparr said.

"I assume you're no longer considering him AWOL," I said.

Sparr shook his head. "No. Under the circumstances, I consider that case closed."

"So, what gets done about the general?" Raymond asked.

"Not much, I'm afraid," Sparr said. "I can't prove he's done anything wrong, and I'm not about to go on a fishing expedition where a one-star's involved."

"I think there is something we can do," I said to Raymond. "But, I need you to get me into see the general."

"He's not likely to agree to meet you."

He had a point, but there's always a plan B. "True," I said. "But, you don't need an appointment to see him, do you?"

He picked up on my meaning right away. "Right. And I can escort you into the Pentagon." He smiled broadly.

"Then, what are we waiting for. Let's go see him."

"In the meantime," Sparr said. "Lila Thissen, I'm placing you under arrest for conspiracy in the kidnapping of Sergeant Lake." He took out a pair of cuffs and none too gently spun her around to put them on. "You have the right to remain silent. But, if you give up that right, anything you say can be used against you in a court of law. You have the right to an attorney. If you cannot afford an attorney, one will be appointed for you. And, you have the right to have your attorney present at any-"

"Yeah, yeah, I understand," she said. "I have my own attorney, and I won't be answering any of your questions until he's present." She glared at him, and then turned to Alec Sweeney who had been standing by with his mouth agape during the entire proceedings. "Alec, would you notify Vincent, and have him meet us wherever this ape's taking me."

I had to give her credit. All the cards were stacked against her, but she'd regained some of her composure. She would be a far harder nut to crack than her henchman Morgan

Freer had been. As Sparr escorted her toward the elevator, she walked with her shoulder's back and her head held high. The door to Haydn Winchester's office was open and he stood there with a puzzled look on his face. I think he sensed that his house of cards was about to tumble.

Charles Ray

32.

We drove back to my office where Raymond and Lake retrieved their pickups, and then drove to the Pentagon. Since the attack, no visitor parking had been allowed. I had to park at the Pentagon City Mall, south of I-395, and walk to the South Entrance of the Pentagon, which was about three-quarters of a mile away. Raymond and Lake were waiting for me at the checkpoint outside the building, where an armed member of the Pentagon police force checked their building passes and military IDs, and then insisted on seeing two picture IDs for me. He frowned when I showed him my PI license and driver's license, but grunted and waved us through.

Once inside, we had to go through another identification procedure at the visitor's center, where I was photographed and issued a plastic badge that I was warned to wear prominently displayed at all times while inside the building. The words 'ESCORT REQUIRED' were displayed in large red letters beneath my photo. Security had tightened considerably since my last visit to the building, when all I had to do was exit the subway train, and take the escalator up to the checkpoint inside the building, where I didn't need an escort to get a pass to enter the building.

As we passed yet another security checkpoint, where our badges were scanned, and took an escalator up a level, I saw scaffolds and workmen all over. The place was as crowded as it usually had been when I visited, but there was a subdued mood that I hadn't noticed before. There were large posters up memorializing those who'd died in the attack, and a number of the hallways to our left were still blocked off. Somehow, this made the attacks of September 11 finally real for me. I felt an intense sadness and a bit of anger as we walked from the outer E Ring to Raymond's office in C Ring.

The Pentagon looks impressive from the outside, its massive walls squatting overlooking the Potomac River, and when you walk the corridors, it's impressive, with the paintings and photos of battle scenes, famous military heroes, and military memorabilia. But, the offices of all but the senior civilians or military with stars on their collars are typical military-issue cubby holes with metal GI desks, no windows except the outermost offices of the different rings, which are usually reserved for high ranking non-general officer types, which Raymond was not. His office was only slightly larger than mine, and it was accessed through an even smaller entry room in which a young female corporal manned a desk and phone. She smiled at us as we tramped past.

He had two extra chairs, but the place was so cramped I wasn't tempted to sit. I stood near the door, propped against a metal bookcase in which he kept military manuals and procurement magazines. The usual array of certificates, awards, and photos lined the wall behind his desk.

He checked his inbox quickly, and flipped everything to the outbox. "Okay," he said. "Let's go see the general."

We trooped out, Raymond leading, me in the middle, and Sergeant Lake bringing up the rear. Even though Bennington's office was only two rings over, it was on the far side of the building, which was a good hike, part way around the E Ring, across two rings, and then more hiking once we got to C Ring.

Bennington's outer office was manned by a captain and a master sergeant, befitting his rank. The captain sat stiffly erect when he looked up and saw Raymond enter. The master sergeant was banging away at an electric typewriter, and ignored us.

"Colonel Raymond," the captain said,

looking strangely at me. "Are you here to see the general?"

"Yes, and it's urgent," Raymond answered. He didn't break stride as he walked past the captain's desk and reached for the door handle.

The young captain looked as if wanted to stop us, but in the military hierarchy lieutenant colonels are not normally challenged by captains, at least not captains who'd like to make major. He tactfully looked away as Raymond pushed the door open.

Bennington's office had more space than mine and Heather's combined. He sat behind a large mahogany desk in a luxurious leather chair. A large credenza that spanned the wall was behind him, and on it were silver trays, plastic and glass trophies and an assortment of coins and medals. Four high back chairs sat in a row in front of the desk. From the entrance to his desk was at least twenty feet, and it was covered with a lush maroon carpet with the army crest embroidered in it. To the right and left were low bookcases with leather bound volumes, and to the right was a window with a view of an identical window in the B Ring. As a one-star, he didn't rate an office with a view of the river or Arlington Cemetery, or like some two-stars I knew, a view of the courtyard in the center of the building.

Except for a telephone and two empty trays to either side of him, his desk was empty.

He looked up as we crossed the room, his brow wrinkling. He frowned deeply when he looked at me.

"Bill, have a seat," he said. "You too, Sergeant Lake. I just got a call from DIS. Glad to hear you weren't AWOL, and sorry to hear about your ordeal." He gave me a curious look. "And, you sir? I don't believe we've been introduced."

I noticed that he hadn't invited me to sit.

"Sir," Raymond said. "This is Al Pennyback. He's a retired army colonel who now works as a private investigator here in DC. It was he who rescued Sergeant Lake."

"Well, in that case, Mr. Pennyback," Bennington said. "I guess we owe you a debt of gratitude."

"He did more than just rescue the sergeant," Raymond said. "He also obtained proof that Armcor was, as Sergeant Lake previously reported, faking test results and defrauding the government."

Bennington looked down at his hands, and then he looked up at Lake with a piercing gaze. "Are you sure about this, sergeant? This is a serious matter. We can't just blithely accuse a respected company of wrongdoing, you know."

"Yes, sir," Lake said forcefully. "I'm absolutely sure."

"I think the fact that Lila Thissen of Armcor had the sergeant kidnapped and tortured to find out what he knew is proof enough that his allegations are well founded," I said.

Bennington's mouth opened, and his eyes blinked rapidly. "Wha-"

"Thanks to you, general, Thissen got her hands on the sergeant's original notes and destroyed them," I went on. "Unfortunately for her, I'd made photographic copies, which a lawyer friend of mine assures me are as good as the original as long as the sergeant can certify they are photos of his notes . . . which he does."

"Uh, well, yes . . . I suppose that would make a difference." Beads of sweat broke out on his broad forehead.

"Yes, sir," Raymond said. "And, thankfully, Al rescued Rory before his abductor could kill him, which is what he was about to do—at the orders of Lila Thissen."

Bennington's face paled. His mouth opened and closed. He looked like he was about to have a heart attack or stroke.

"I got the kidnapper to talk before turning him over to the cops," I said. "It turns out that he was the one who told Thissen about the notes in the magazine. Before then, I'd thought you were the one who told her."

"What? How dare you accuse me of such a thing," Bennington said. Some color was coming back to his cheeks.

"Come on, general, you're no fool. You

had to know Armcor wasn't qualified for that contract, and when Bill here informed you that your man on site observed wrongdoing, you knew he wasn't wrong. You've been protecting them despite their lack of qualification. Lila Thissen's been arrested, and the whole mess is gonna come out in the open."

"W-why would I do such a thing? It's my job to get the best possible equipment for our troops."

"Yeah, but this piece of crap Armcor's trying to sell the government is just that," I said. "But, I know why you did it."

"Yes, why is that?"

I was tempted to just blurt it out. Raymond already knew, but Lake didn't. Bennington was a corrupt political general who didn't deserve any respect, but I have my limits. I'd give him a way out.

"It has to do with certain trips to New York and Philadelphia," I said. "I was able to find out about them, and I have no doubt that Armcor did as well. Am I right?"

He swallowed; his Adam's apple bobbing up and down. "Uh, there's a good-"

"No, general, there's not really. But, with Thissen in jail, and I think she'll be there for a good long time, you have no reason not to cancel the contract and let someone do it that is qualified. I don't think Armcor would dare bring up the trips under the present circumstances."

He looked desperate, a drowning man who'd just been tossed a lifeline. Our eyes met. He knew what I was doing for him. What I wanted to do was smash his face in.

"One other thing, general," I went on. "I think you should probably recuse yourself from any further involvement in this program, don't you agree?"

A defiant look briefly flashed in his eyes, but he knew when he was beaten. My expression conveyed that. I was willing to let him retain a bit of honor, but not get a free ride.

"Yes, Mr. Pennyback. I think you're right. I'm due for retirement soon anyway. Colonel Raymond, effective immediately you're in charge of the program until they can find someone to replace me."

He stood and, his shoulders slumped, walked to the door. "Captain Carter," he said after he opened the door. "Could you come in, please?"

I stood. "Well, gentlemen," I said. "I think we should leave."

Raymond and Lake followed me back to the corridor. As we headed back to Raymond's office, Lake walked up beside me.

"Mr. Pennyback, what the hell just happened back there?"

I smiled and patted him on the shoulder. "Sergeant, there are some things it's best not knowing. Let's just say, that order has been returned to the universe, and karma is once again balanced."

Lake looked befuddled. He shot an imploring look at Raymond.

"Don't ask, sergeant," he said. "You probably wouldn't understand anyway. Let's just say that Mr. Pennyback here is a man who can get things done that we mere mortals can't even begin to fathom and let it go at that."

Lake made a growling sound deep in his throat. "I'll never understand you officers."

Charles Ray

33.

Raymond sent a check a few days later for services rendered, along with a fulsome thank you note. I slipped the note in my desk drawer and gave Heather the check to deposit to our account.

"The one thing I really like about military guys," she said. "Is that they pay their debts on time."

"Most do," I said. "And, the ones that don't get into a world of trouble. Courts martial are a lot tougher than dunning notices." I stood up and headed for the door.

"Where are you going?"

"I owe Quincy an explanation of what happened in exchange for the help he gave me. Be back in a couple hours."

Quincy's blue-haired assistant made a

face at me as I walked up to her desk. "Where's that hunk who was with you the other day?" she asked.

"Back at work," I said. "But, when I see him, I'll tell him you asked about him. Is Quincy free . . . I need a few minutes of his time?"

She held up a well-manicured right index finger, and pushed the intercom switch on her phone with the left.

"Yes?" Quincy's cultured voice came over the little speaker.

"Al would like to come in and talk to you for a few minutes, Quincy," she said.

"Sure, send him in."

Another poke of her finger, and the connection was severed with a click. "Go on in," she said.

Quincy, jacketless and without a vest today, sat behind his desk. A legal-sized blue folder lay open before him. When I approached his desk, he sighed wearily and closed the folder.

"Hope I'm not interrupting anything important," I said.

He stabbed the folder and frowned. "Reading legal briefs is seldom important, and never fun," he said. "What can I do for you, Al?"

I flopped in the chair next to his desk. "You were a big help in my last case, so I thought I'd fill you in on what happened."

"I saw the news reports about Lila

Thissen's arrest," he said. "It didn't go into too many details, but from what they did print, she was a ba-a-a-ad girl."

"That, my friend, is an understatement. She got wind that Sergeant Lake, the guy monitoring the drone project for the Pentagon, suspected the company was cooking test results, so she hired this thug, Morgan Freer, to make friends with him and find out what he knew."

"According to the papers, Freer has a rap sheet for assault, drug dealing, and assorted other bad behavior going back to his teens," he said. "How did someone like Lila Thissen hook up with him?"

"Apparently Thissen and her boss, Haydn Winchester, know a lot of shady types," I said. "They hired some fly-by-night gumshoe to look into their competition and assorted officials at the Pentagon, looking for dirt they could use to boost their chances during contract bids."

He shook his head. "That's not typical behavior for defense contractors, but, I guess every barrel has its share of rotten apples."

"What's really bad," I said. "Is the fact that Thissen was willing to go to the wire to get what she wanted—including ordering the kidnapping and murder of Rory Lake."

"It's a good thing you found him when you did."

It had been close, too close for my money. A few seconds later and I'd have found Lake with his throat slashed.

"Yeah," I said. "Thissen and Freer will spend a long time behind bars for that little caper. Special Agent Sparr called me to tell me they're falling all over themselves trying to make deals with the feds. Every day, one of them reveals some more damning information about the other."

"I hope the U.S. Attorney's not gonna allow either of them to plea bargain their way out of this."

I sighed. That, unfortunately, was the way the justice system worked. The only good thing about it was that there was enough evidence on both of them for such a variety of offenses, pleading out on one wouldn't absolve them of the others.

"I'm keeping my fingers crossed. I think the Justice Department's pissed enough to take a hard line with both of 'em. I just hope this is a wake-up call for the brass at the Pentagon, and they watch these contractors a little closer."

"I wouldn't hold my breath on that one," he said. "I have some friends working on the Joint Staff, and while they won't give me details, the scuttlebutt they do pass along says we're about to go to war. When that happens, there's likely to be less rather than more oversight."

"War? Who the hell are we planning to fight now?"

Quincy laughed. "Al, Al, you really need

to pay more attention to what's going on in the world."

"You mean, buy a TV or subscribe to a newspaper? Hey, I buy the Sunday *Washington Post* every couple of months, and sometimes I listen to the news on NPR." I hadn't done either for over a month. I find the news shows either depressing or dopey. "The world's full of shitty stuff, and I don't need to bore myself with that to know it."

"Yeah, but it also means you don't know what's going on," he said. "Ever since 9-11, the politicians have been going ape shit, and looking for someone to smash. That bunch in the Middle East, *al Qaeda*, is claiming credit for the attacks, and there's intelligence that the Taliban in Afghanistan has given them bases and safe haven. My buddies say it's a matter of weeks before we send troops to root them out."

"So, we send a few special ops guys in to whack a bunch of terrorists," I said. "That's not the same as war."

He shook his head. "I'm not talking about a few black ops. I'm talking about the whole shebang, air strikes, boots on the ground, the whole bit. My buddy in J-3 says they're talking about hitting the Taliban as well as *al Qaeda*."

I could hardly believe what I was hearing. "We're gonna invade Afghanistan? Hell, folks have been trying that since Hannibal, and getting their clocks cleaned in the process.

Look what happened to the Soviets when they went in in '79. That's why we have fucking *al Qaeda* in the first place. We created that bunch to join the *mujahedeen* to fight the damn Russians."

"Hey, you know politicians are never strong on history," he said. "Right now, they just want to be seen as doing something— even if it's wrong. I hear there's support for strikes in both parties."

"Shit," I said. "Won't we ever learn?"

"That's not the worse part. I'm hearing that some of the real far right types are also talking about going into Iraq to take out Saddam, and a few of the generals are going along with it."

"I might not follow the news, but I know we don't have the forces for a proper invasion of one country, much less two, and two in one of the worse places in the world to send troops."

"Oh, they're planning for that," he said. "They're gonna freeze enlistments, so tours of duty will get extended, and they'll be pulling in reserve and guard units for rotations."

"What the hell is the State Department doing in all this?"

"What do you think?" He had a look of total exasperation. "From what I hear, the folks over at Foggy Bottom have been completely cut out of the decision chain on this. Hell, a buddy of mine said someone at State sent over a paper on an exit strategy for

Afghanistan, and it was shredded."

"You've got to be kidding. The generals are gonna send troops in to fight with no plans for what to do when the shooting stops?"

"Yeah, looks that way. The way my friend described it, they plan to go in, kick the shit out of everything that moves, and come home."

I couldn't resist rolling my eyes. "And, you think I should pay more attention to the news? If that's what's being put out, I'll stay ignorant, thanks. Shit, this'll make Korea and Vietnam look like great strategic thinking. Man, aren't you glad you're no longer in uniform?"

He looked wistful. "Yeah, sort of . . . but, a lot of guys I know are gonna get caught up in this meat grinder. I feel kinda guilty not being there with 'em."

I knew how he felt. "I know," I said. "Sometimes I feel the same way."

34.

I was feeling glum when I left Quincy's office. I'd solved the case satisfactorily, and saved a life in the process. But, Rory Lake was a soldier, and if we went to war, he'd be among the first to go. I knew his type. He wouldn't wait to be ordered to go—he'd volunteer. So, for that matter, would Bill Raymond. I knew this, because when I was in their shoes, I would have done the same. It didn't matter that it was a fool's errand, if my unit was going to war, I went along. Not because of some hyper-sense of patriotism or respect for the politicians who start the damn wars, but because of a sense of duty to the individuals with whom I served. Soldiers don't go to war for medals, or because they like to fight. They go because of the bond they share with other soldiers.

There was nothing I could do about it, though. Maybe Quincy was right. Maybe I did need to stay more tuned in to the crap going on around me. I hated the thought of listening to the news on TV or radio, except for a lot of the stuff on NPR. They, at least, covered the stuff the main stream outlets ignored, and didn't slant or try to convert it into entertainment as so many did. I'd long ago given up on newspapers. I bought a Sunday paper occasionally for the comics and the Sunday puzzles. The front page, sports, editorial page, and the rest, which was mostly ads anyway, went into the recycle bin. I know that a good citizen is an informed citizen, and cutting myself off from the news might seem to indicate that I'm not a good citizen. But, the news had long ago ceased to inform. For me, it was like organized religion. I wasn't sure where I stood on the whole question of an afterlife, but I knew damn well that most of what passed for organized religion didn't have a clue either, so I cut out the middle man.

Such heavy thoughts before lunch were guaranteed to give me an upset stomach, so as I breezed into the office, I decided it was time to find some kind of diversion. Maybe a visit to Blood Raine's place to return his camera and have some of his great coffee.

Heather was sitting at her desk looking at her computer screen. For a change she wasn't typing.

"Hey, Heather," I said. "I'm thinking about bagging it early today. I think I'll take off and go have lunch with Blood. Can you cover the office by yourself for the rest of the day?"

She looked up at me. There was a slightly unfocused look in her eyes.

"Yeah, I could cover, but I have a better idea," she said. "Why don't we both take the rest of the day off?"

I shook my head. I was not hearing workaholic Heather Bunche talking about leaving the office early.

"*You* want to take time off? I don't think I've ever heard you say that. What do you plan to do?"

She hesitated. Her cheeks reddened, and she looked down. "Well, it's like this," she said. "Rory . . . Sergeant Lake called. He's been given a few days off to recuperate from his ordeal, and he wondered if I'd like to go on a picnic with him. I was planning to ask for the rest of the day off, but since you want to take off too, I think we should just close the office and have some fun."

Karmic balance, Yin and Yang, the inevitable order of the Universe—call it what you will, but the world always seems to find the middle path. Whenever things get out of kilter in one corner of the universe, they fall into place in another. The look on Heather's cherubic face wiped the negative thoughts from my mind.

"That, partner, sounds like a plan," I said.

I turned and walked out of the office. Heather was already shutting down her computer and humming an unrecognizable tune. I could feel the smile on my own face.

Books by Charles Ray

Al Pennyback mysteries

Color Me Dead
Memorial to the Dead
Deadline
Dead, White, and Blue
A Good Day to Die
The Day the Music Died
Die, Sinner
Deadly Intentions
Death by Design
Till Death Do Us Part
Deadly Dose
Dead Man's Cove
Dead Men Don't Answer
Deadly Paradise
Kiss of Death
Death in White Satin
Death and Taxis
Drop Dead, Gorgeous
Deadbeat
A Deadly Wind Blows
Death Wish

The Buffalo Soldier series:

Trial by Fire
Homecoming
Incident at Cactus Junction
Peacekeepers
Renegade

Escort Duty
Battle at Dead Man's Gulch
Yosemite
Comanchero
Range War

Other fiction

Angel on His Shoulder
She's No Angel
Child of the Flame
Pip's Revenge
Wallace in Underland
Further Adventures of Wallace in Underland
Dead Letter and Other Tales
The White Dragons
The Dragon's Lair
Dragon Slayer
The Last Gunfighters
The Culling
Frontier Justice: Bass Reeves, Deputy U.S. Marshal
Angel on His Shoulder – Revised Edition

Nonfiction

Things I Learned from My Grandmother About Leadership and Life
Taking Charge: Effective Leadership for the Twenty-first Century
Grab the Brass Ring

There's Always A Plan B
African Places: A Photographic Journey
   Through Zimbabwe and southern Africa
A Portrait of Africa
In the Line of Fire: American Diplomats in
   the Trenches

Children's books

The Yak and the Yeti
Samantha and the Bully
Molly Learns to Share

Charles Ray

About the Author

Charles Ray has been writing fiction since his teens. He won a Sunday school magazine writing contest when he was thirteen, and having his byline on a short story published in a national publication forever hooked him on writing. During his time in the army (1962-1982) he often moonlighted as a newspaper or magazine journalist, and was the editorial cartoonist for the Spring Lake (NC) News, a weekly newspaper, during the 1970s. In addition to his writing, he was an artist/cartoonist and photographer for a number of publications, including Ebony, Eagle and Swan, and Essence, and had a monthly cartoon feature and did several covers for Buffalo, a now-defunct magazine that was dedicated to showcasing the contributions of African-Americans to the country's military history.

After retiring from the army, he joined the U.S. Foreign Service, and served as a diplomat in posts in Asia and Africa until his retirement in 2012. He has worked and traveled throughout the world (Antarctica is the only continent he hasn't visited), and now, as a full time writer, continues to globetrot looking for interesting things to write about, draw, or take pictures of.

A native of Texas, he now calls Maryland home. For more on his writing and other projects, check the following Web sites:

http://charlesaray.blogspot.com
http://charlieray45.wordpress.com
http://www.twitter.com/charlieray45
http://www.facebook.com/charlieray45
http://www.flickr.com/photos/charlesray45/
http://www.viewbug.com/member/charlesray
https://unsplash.com/Charles_Ray
http://fineartamerica.com/profiles/2-charles-ray.html
https://www.facebook.com/UhuruPressbooks

www.ingramcontent.com/pod-product-compliance
Lightning Source LLC
Chambersburg PA
CBHW071503170626
46811CB00007B/2713